Volume III

by Tony Abbott

SCHOLASTIC INC.
New York Toronto London Auckland Sydney
Mexico City New Delhi Hong Kong Buenos Aires

No part of this publication may be reproduced, stored in a retrieval system, or transmitted in any form or by any means, electronic, mechanical, photocopying, recording, or otherwise, without written permission of the publisher. For information regarding permission, write to Scholastic Inc., Attention: Permissions Department, 557 Broadway, New York, NY 10012.

The Tower of the Elf King, ISBN 0-439-20772-X
Text copyright © 2000 by Robert T. Abbott.
Book design by Dawn Adelman.

Quest for the Queen, ISBN 0-439-20784-3
Text copyright © 2000 by Robert T. Abbott.
Illustrations copyright © 2000 by Scholastic Inc.
Book design by Dawn Adelman.

The Hawk Bandits of Tarkoom, ISBN 0-439-20785-1
Text copyright © 2001 by Robert T. Abbott.
Book design by Dawn Adelman.

Under the Serpent Sea, ISBN 0-439-20786-X
Text copyright © 2001 by Robert T. Abbott.
Illustrations copyright © 2001 by Scholastic Inc.
Book design by Dawn Adelman.

All rights reserved. Published by Scholastic Inc. SCHOLASTIC and associated logos are trademarks and/or registered trademarks of Scholastic Inc.

12 11 10 9 8 7 6 5 4 3 2 1   5 6 7 8 9 10/0

Printed in the U.S.A.   40

This edition created exclusively for Barnes & Noble, Inc.

2005 Barnes & Noble Books

ISBN 0-7607-9583-5

First compilation printing, August 2005

Contents

The Tower of
the Elf King

To my parents,
for making a house where books ruled

One

Dream Pictures

"Hey, Eric! Watch me!"

Eric Hinkle looked up in time to see his friend Neal do a cannonball into his backyard pool.

Splash!

It was hot and sunny in Neal's backyard. His parents were having a big cookout. Everyone was laughing, swimming, and eating.

But Eric couldn't get into it. All he could

think about was a dream he'd had last night.

A dream about . . . Droon.

Ssss! Neal's mother set a pot of bubbling chili on the grill. Then she loaded on some hot dogs.

Droon was the magical world Eric and his friends Neal and Julie had discovered while cleaning up Eric's basement one day.

They'd found a small empty closet. As soon as they went inside — *whoosh!* — the floor vanished and a staircase appeared.

A staircase to the wonderful world of Droon.

Droon was a land of awesome adventure. A land of excitement.

And sometimes danger. But Eric loved it.

He, Julie, and Neal had made good friends in Droon. One was a princess named Keeah. Another was a wizard named Galen. Together, they were fighting a wicked sorcerer named Lord Sparr. The kids were helping them make sure Sparr didn't take over Droon.

After each visit, the kids couldn't wait to go back. Sometimes, when Keeah needed help, she sent a message through an enchanted soccer ball. Other times, the kids dreamed about Droon. That's how they knew when to return.

But this time, Eric wasn't so sure he wanted to return. He'd seen a face in his dream.

The face of something terrifying.

The first thing he did when he woke up was draw a picture of it.

Now he had to show the picture to his friends. But no one else could see. Droon was a secret.

"Hey, Neal!" Eric called out. "Where's Julie?"

"Coming soon!" Then Neal did a goofy dive and flopped into the water on his stomach.

Eric looked around. No one was watching, so he pulled out the picture and stared at it.

It stared right back.

With three angry red eyes.

"Not even Sparr has three eyes!" he mumbled.

"Chili dog?" asked a voice over his shoulder.

Eric quickly covered the paper. "No, thanks," he said. Then he looked up. "Julie!"

Julie was in a T-shirt and shorts. She sat down at the picnic table and began chomping on her hot dog. "Why aren't you in the pool?"

"I dreamed about Droon last night," Eric said. "But the only thing I remember is . . . this."

He showed Julie the drawing.

Julie nearly dropped her food. "Oh, my gosh! You made a drawing, too?"

She pulled a sheet of paper from her pocket and placed it on the table next to Eric's picture.

Eric blinked. "And I thought mine was scary!"

Julie's drawing showed a mouth with two rows of long teeth sticking out. But the teeth weren't the worst part. The worst part was the fire pouring out between them.

Neal came splashing over to the table, drying himself with a towel. "What's this, art class?"

"Scary art class," said Julie. "Take a look. Here's what we've been dreaming about."

"Whoa, a three-eyed monster eating my mom's extra-hot chili!" said Neal with a laugh.

"Yeah," whispered Eric. "All we need is a nose and we've got the creepiest monster ever!"

Neal stopped laughing. "You know what's weird? I dreamed about a nose last night."

Eric jumped up from the table. "Draw it right now. This is important. It could be a clue to what's happening in Droon!"

"I don't draw too well," said Neal. He looked around. "But the nose looked like . . . this!"

He took four chocolate chip cookies from the dessert plate and stacked them between the drawings. "That's the nose."

Eric frowned. "It looks like a pig nose."

"Exactly!" said Neal. "With three nostrils. It was huffing and puffing. It sneezed a lot, too."

"That's not very scary," said Julie.

"Did I mention the nose was drippy?" he added.

"That's it!" said Eric. "We need to go to Droon right now!" He stuffed the pictures in his pocket.

Neal snatched the cookies.

"Don't hog the food, son!" his father called.

"I'll share!" Neal said. Then he ran into the house to change. Two minutes later they were all at Eric's back door.

"You know what I think is cool?" asked Julie as they entered Eric's house.

"That we can spend all day in Droon and still be back in time for chili dogs?" said Neal.

"Besides that," said Julie. "It means we're a team. It took all of us together to figure out that there's some kind of monster in Droon."

"And that we need to go back," Eric added, charging through the kitchen and down to the basement. It was still pretty messy there. They never did finish cleaning it up.

Someday we'll get to it, Eric thought. Then he grinned. *But not today!*

They quickly pulled aside the cartons that blocked the little door under the basement stairs.

Neal opened the door. Inside was a small closet, completely bare except for a single light hanging from the ceiling. The three kids piled in.

"Ready to face the monster?" Eric asked.

Julie smiled. "Ready."

Click! Neal flicked off the light.

Whoosh! The floor below them vanished. They were standing on the top step of a long, glimmering staircase. The staircase to Droon.

As they started down, Eric recalled that Droon and his world — the Upper World — were connected by more than a magical staircase.

On their last adventure, Princess Keeah had come into Eric's basement for a minute. Then she said she had been there before!

Talk about secrets!

Galen had told them the staircase had been sealed for many years before the kids found it. So what did Keeah mean that she had been to the Upper World before? When? How? Why?

This time, Eric would ask her.

The stairs curved through a thin layer of pink clouds. The sky below was turning purple. It was the end of the day in Droon.

Neal peered down the stairs. "Hey! I

should have kept my trunks on, after all. There's a swimming pool down there —"

Suddenly, the stairs began to wobble.

"Uh-oh," said Julie. "Should we go back up?"

The stairs shivered and quivered.

"We can't!" Eric said. "Hurry, or we'll fall off."

They rushed down the steps two at a time.

"Prepare to dive!" said Neal.

Then Eric squinted over Neal's shoulder.

"Wait! That's not a swimming pool," he said.

"It's not?" said Neal, leaning forward.

Below them sat a giant cauldron, boiling fiercely. Red and blue flames licked up the sides.

"It's more like . . . a pot of chili!" cried Julie.

"I hope the cook isn't Lord Sparr!" Neal said.

Then — *whoosh!* — the stairs vanished.

The three friends fell through the air, straight toward the boiling pot.

"Help!" Eric screamed.

Hiss! Bubble! Splort! went the pot.

Two

The Ceremony of Truth

Zamm! A sudden blue light sizzled over the kids. They stopped falling. They stopped moving. They hung just inches above the hissing pot.

"Are we . . . cooked?" asked Neal.

"I don't think so," said Julie.

"This cauldron is on some kind of balcony," said Eric. "And it looks like there's a castle behind us —"

"My friends!" called a bright voice.

It was Princess Keeah. She ran across the stone balcony toward the kids. She was dressed in a blue tunic with a golden belt. A crown circled her head.

"You nearly became part of our spell!" she said. "I stopped you with only seconds to spare."

"Hey, I was just hoping we weren't the secret ingredient in Sparr's evil soup," Neal said.

A roar of laughter came from the castle. It was the warm voice of Galen Longbeard, first wizard of Droon. "It's not soup," he said. "It's not Sparr's. And it's certainly not to be eaten!"

Together with Keeah, Galen raised his hands and — *zzz!* — more blue light fell over the kids. They floated to the ground beside the pot.

Eric looked around. "We're in Jaffa City."

Keeah nodded. "This is the balcony outside my room. Galen and I are in the middle of an ancient spell called the Ceremony of Truth. We're using it to find out what happened to Sparr."

Eric glanced at his friends. "What do you mean?" he asked. "Is Sparr . . . missing?"

Keeah nodded slowly. "For nearly a whole moon no one has seen him. We're hoping that he won't bother us anymore. But we can't be sure until we find out where he is."

Eric remembered the last time he'd seen the wicked sorcerer. Sparr had been lying on the frozen lake near his evil fortress of Plud. He had been hurt.

But even in his pain, Sparr had stared up at Eric with eyes that said, *It is not over. Not over.*

Hsss! The cauldron began to hiss wildly.

Galen leaned over and sniffed the pot. "It is ready. Keeah, as part of your wizard training, would you do the honors?"

"Yes, sir!" she said brightly.

"Ready, Max?" Galen called over the side of the balcony to his assistant.

Max, an orange-haired spider troll, stood on the ground below. With his eight legs, he was holding up a large round board painted with brightly colored circles like a target.

"Ready, master!" he chirped.

At once, Keeah took a large ladle and thrust it into the boiling pot. When she lifted it out, it was thick with long white strands.

Julie nudged Eric. "That looks like spaghetti!"

Keeah went to the edge of the balcony and flung the goop off the ladle.

It fell through the air and — *splat!* — struck the target in the center.

"Direct hit!" Max chirped.

"Everyone, hurry!" said Keeah excitedly.

They all raced down to the courtyard.

Galen peered at the target. "Is he there?"

Julie asked, "Is *who* there?"

"Lord Sparr," Keeah said, leaning over. "Galen is looking for his face in the strands."

"There! A shape!" Max chirped. "I'd know those ear fins anywhere!"

Galen squinted at the blob. Then he sniffed it and walked completely around it. "Yes, it is Sparr," he said finally, poking the white stringy strands. "He is somewhere in the dark lands. But it's not clear what he is up to."

Neal nudged Eric. "A spaghetti Sparr? Makes me think of meatballs. . . ."

"Those are the Ninns!" Julie said with a laugh.

The Ninns were Sparr's plump, red-faced warriors. They were slow-witted and always angry.

"Is this actually *magic*?" Eric asked.

Galen laughed. "An ancient form of it, yes. You make a mess, but sometimes it works."

"If we learn that Sparr is gone, I'll happily clean up!" added Max as he pulled some white strands from his thick orange hair.

"Wow," said Julie. "What if it is true? If Sparr really is gone, wouldn't Droon be at peace?"

Galen smiled sadly. "So you would think. But the Ninns are leaving his dark lands in vast numbers. Something is up."

"Also, we've heard rumors about dangerous new creatures roaming Droon," said Keeah.

Eric looked at Julie and Neal. "New creatures? I almost forgot!" He pulled the drawings from his pocket and held them together. "Something like this?"

"How scary!" said Keeah.

"It has a nose, too," said Julie. "Neal, show them the cookies. We need the whole picture."

"The cookies?" Neal grinned. "Well, I, uh, sort of ate them. On the stairs. I was hungry!"

Julie narrowed her eyes at him. "Anyway, the monster had a pig nose."

"A pig nose . . ." Galen said. He gave the pictures, then the kids, a quizzical look. "I've never seen anything like it. Not in all of Droon."

"And that," Max chimed in, "is saying a

lot! My master Galen has seen nearly every beast —"

Blam! Blam! The giant gates of Jaffa City rocked. Someone was pounding on them.

"Help!" came a cry from outside the walls.

The palace guards opened the gates at once. Before them stood a small purple creature that looked a lot like a pillow.

"It's Khan!" said Max. "King of the Lumpies!"

Everyone ran over as Khan staggered in.

"M-my . . . village . . ." he stammered. "It's been robbed! By a fire-breathing monster! A monster with . . . three eyes!"

Three

The Plundered Village

Eric and Julie rushed to show Khan their drawings.

"It's him!" said the Lumpy king as he rested on the palace steps. "I saw the monster for only a moment. But those eyes! I'll never forget them!"

"Calm yourself, my dear Khan," Galen said.

"I can't be calm!" he replied. "Even my

beautiful crown was stolen. The legendary treasure of the Lumpies is gone. All the gold and jewels passed down from Lumpy to Lumpy since the beginnings of Droon. All of it, stolen in the dead of night."

The tassels on Khan's shoulders slumped as he spoke. Eric had never seen Khan so sad.

"We'll help you find your treasure," Eric said firmly. "I think it's why we're here. We dreamed of this monster. So we'll find him and get your treasure back. Right?"

Julie and Neal nodded.

"Galen?" said Keeah. "May I go, too?"

The wizard stroked his beard. "Yes, all of you should go. Keeah, take your magic harp. But be careful. We still don't know all of its powers."

"Yes, sir," she said.

Galen turned on his heels. "Max, get

the target. We'll try the Ceremony of Truth again. We will get to the bottom of this problem yet!"

As Galen and Max strode away, the princess called out, "Magic harp . . . come to me!"

Instantly, a dark shape flew out from her window high above them. It circled the balcony once, then landed gently in Keeah's arms.

"Awesome!" said Eric. "Now *that* is magic."

The instrument was called a bowharp. Shaped like a U, it bore two sets of strings crossing each other. It had once belonged to Keeah's mother, Queen Relna. But Keeah hadn't had it for long, and she still didn't know everything it could do.

"Galen told me that the harp was made by someone called the Maker," said Keeah as she slung it over her shoulder. "No one has seen him for years. But I'll show you one thing I discovered. Is everyone ready to go?"

Khan and the kids nodded.

"Then hold still," said Keeah. She spoke some strange words, then plucked the harp strings — *pling! blong!* Suddenly a rosy light beamed from the harp and fell over them all. The air quivered around the children.

"It feels like we're moving," said Julie.

"We are!" said Keeah. Then *plang!* — the song ended, the rosy light vanished, and they found themselves at the walls of a village surrounded by sand.

"Awesome!" said Neal. "Where are we now?"

"The deserts of Lumpland," said Keeah. "The scene of the crime. Where we might find clues to where the monster went next."

Khan led them into the village just as the sun vanished below the horizon and the first stars began twinkling in the sky.

The Lumpies' houses were made of dried mud and were stacked one on top of the other.

"The robbers came while we were sleeping," the king said. "They stole everything. Jewels, gold, silver. Even our kitchen utensils!"

"How greedy can a monster be?" asked Neal.

"Indeed," Khan went on. "Try cooking without pots and pans! Very messy business!"

They passed down one narrow street after another. Here and there were broken windows. Even the street lamps were dark.

"They stole your streetlights?" asked Julie.

"The silver lamps of my grandmother

once used to light our way," Khan said. "But not anymore!"

Finally, the king brought them to his own house. He called it his palace, but it wasn't much larger than the other Lumpies' homes.

Khan pointed to a hole in the front door. "Look, even my copper doorknob was taken!"

Inside, Khan showed them his sleeping chamber, then turned away.

"The sight of it makes me weak," he said.

A small stand next to the bed lay empty.

"I took off my crown last night and put it there, as I always do," Khan said. "Later, there was a noise and I awoke. It was dark, but I saw the monster. We tussled, but he took the crown. Then he and his helpers raced away."

"You're sure the Ninns didn't do this?" Eric asked. "Galen said they're popping up all over Droon."

Khan shook his head. "The Ninns have simple minds," he replied. "They need someone to lead them. Besides, no Ninn has three fiery eyes. This creature was different."

"Speaking of different," said Julie, "what's this?" From the floor she picked up a flat green object the size and shape of a coin.

"It looks like a scale from the monster's skin!" said Khan. He sniffed it. "Yes! I know the smell! Good work, Julie. We can use this scale to track him down!"

Without another word, Khan shot straight out of his house. The kids followed him.

A pale half moon had risen over the village. It cast a silvery light over the desert sand.

"How are we going to track the monster?" said Eric. "This desert is huge."

"You forget what made the Lumpies famous!" Khan said. With a wink he sniffed the small green scale, then pushed his nose into the air. *Sniff! Sniff!*

"The scent is faint, but still there," Khan said, squinting out over the dunes. Then he pointed. "That way. We must follow!"

Ten minutes later, the small troop set out.

Khan took the lead. He stopped every now and then to sniff the scale, then picked up the trail again.

After nearly an hour of trudging across the moonlit sands, they stopped to rest behind a huge sand dune.

While Khan passed a canteen to Julie and Neal, Keeah practiced softly on her harp.

"I think I'll try to see what's out there," Eric said. He stepped away from the camp.

"We'll start soon," said Keeah. "Don't go far."

"Okay," he said. Then he stopped. "Keeah?"

She looked up from her harp. "Yes?"

"Well . . . you said you were in the Upper World before. Was that true? I mean, how?"

The princess shrugged her shoulders slightly. "It's a mystery," she said. "When I saw the trees outside your basement, I just knew I had been there before. I don't know how. I don't know when. But my father says it's impossible."

Eric took a deep breath. "Maybe your mother knows. I mean, you found her magic harp. Maybe it means you'll find her soon, too."

Keeah smiled. "I hope I will."

Keeah's mother, Queen Relna, was under a spell. First she had been a falcon, then a dragon. But where she was now and what form she was in, no one knew.

Eric left Keeah and climbed alone to the top of the dune. Looking up, he saw billions of bright stars twinkling in every direction.

Then something twinkled down below, too.

Eric lowered his gaze. "Holy crow!" he gasped.

At the bottom of the dune was a fire.

No . . . many fires. And tents. Hundreds of tents, spreading far into the distance.

An army of tents. Red ones.

"Ninns!" he hissed. "I've got to warn the others!" But as he turned to rush back, the ridge at the top of the dune gave way. He hit the sand and began to roll.

The more he tried to stop himself, the faster he rolled. Over and over he went, faster and faster, until — *whoosh!*

He crashed right through the back of one of the tents and stopped with a thud.

Yellow light flooded over him.

Eric squinted. Then he stared.

Right into the face of a fierce red Ninn!

Four

In the Company of Ninns

Eric gaped at the face before him.

It was a Ninn, all right.

The chubby red cheeks. The sharp chin. The pointed ears that stuck out to the side. The deep-set black eyes the size of marbles.

But this one was different from any other Ninn Eric had ever seen.

This one was wearing a dress!

"What you?" grunted the Ninn, leaning over, nose to nose with Eric.

"Uh . . . I'm Eric?" he answered.

"Humph!" the Ninn grunted. She pulled away and sat down on a rug that lay like a floor over the sand. Before her, a small pot sizzled over a fire. Smoke from the fire wafted up through a hole in the ceiling of the tent.

Eric wondered if he should bolt out of there as soon as possible. But what if she screamed? What if Sparr was right outside? He looked around.

The inside of the tent was lined with sacks and bundles. So it was true, Eric thought. The Ninns *had* been traveling.

Maybe he could find out where.

"Wahh!" came a squeaky sound from behind the Ninn. Eric nearly jumped out of his skin.

A small Ninn, a child of maybe two or three, sat playing quietly behind the woman.

The child already wore the fierce expression of all Ninn warriors.

The Ninn woman scooped a small brown ball from the pot she was stirring. She held it out to the child, who grunted softly, then ate it.

Eric turned to the Ninn. "Is Sparr near here?"

She cast her eyes at the fire under the pot. "Sparr," she grunted. "Sparr . . . gone."

The words sent a shock through him.

"Gone? Sparr *gone*?" he repeated. "Where?"

The Ninn grumbled under her breath as she spooned more food onto a plate.

"Secret place," she said. "No one knows."

"Is he . . . dead?" Eric asked.

"Not dead. Not alive. Now we follow Gryndal."

"Gryndal?" Eric repeated. "Who is he?"

"He worse," the Ninn said. "Lizard. Monster. Gryndal use Ninns to help him build tower."

Eric guessed that the monster was the same one they'd been tracking.

"Gryndal is building a tower?" asked Eric. "Where is it? And what is it for?"

The Ninn grumbled and shrugged her massive shoulders. "Sparr gone. Gryndal worse. Ninns not happy."

For a moment, the only sound was the crackling of the fire. Then there was a grunt from outside. A loud grunt. The tent flap jostled.

"Oh, no!" Eric gasped. "I better go —"

"Be still!" the Ninn woman said. In a flash, she flung a thick blanket over him.

Eric didn't move. He didn't breathe.

Through a small hole in the blanket Eric saw a giant Ninn warrior barrel into the tent as if he lived there.

Then Eric realized . . . he probably did.

The small Ninn yipped once and the warrior patted its fuzzy head. Then the Ninn turned to the woman and growled and grunted strange words. She answered him back the same way.

It was probably the Ninn language, Eric thought. It sounded very strange. Like gargling.

Whatever she said, the warrior didn't seem to like it. He began stomping around the tent, banging things and slapping his hands together.

"Me hungry! Me food . . . now!"

He stared at her, angry and mean-looking.

Suddenly, the woman yelled, "Thalak!"

The warrior bolted upright. He staggered back, his beady eyes squinting at the woman. He grumbled loudly, then — *swoosh!* — the tent flap went up and he was gone.

"Whoa!" whispered Eric. "Saved!"

The woman whipped off the blanket. "Go," she said. "Yak-yak! Far from here. And take."

She held out a small leather sack. Into it she plopped a large helping of the food she'd been cooking on the fire. "Go. Now!"

Wide-eyed, Eric took the sack from the woman. "Thank you. You're very nice."

The woman nodded, then swished her hands at him. Eric scurried back through the tent the way he had come. He climbed back up the dune.

He looked once more at the vast sea of

tents below. Then he slid down the sand to his own little camp. Everyone rushed to him.

"Eric!" cried Keeah. "You gave us such a scare! What happened to you?"

He told them everything.

"The monster's name is Gryndal. The Ninns are building some kind of tower for him. I didn't really understand that part. But the biggest news is that Sparr is gone. At least for now."

Keeah's eyes glimmered. "So it is true. . . ."

"I don't believe it," said Khan with a snarl. "I will never believe it. I can almost smell him."

Neal chuckled. "Unless it's the smell of whatever Eric has in that bag. What is it?"

Eric burst into laughter. "Looks like a Ninn specialty — meatballs!"

Even Khan managed a grin. "But come," he said. "We're wasting time. It's not safe to stay here. Already the scent is growing faint. The monster — and my treasure — are this way!"

Five

Voice of Thunder

The small band trekked through the night.

When morning came they found themselves before a high wall of sand-colored stone.

"Do we stop here?" asked Julie.

Khan shook his head. "No. Gryndal came this way. I'm certain of it."

Keeah scanned the rock. "There is a pass over there," she said, pointing to a

* 43 *

break in the rocks. "We can follow it through to the other side."

The kids headed into the narrow pass. Steep jagged walls rose up on either side. They moved through quietly and in single file.

"This is the perfect place for a sneak attack," Eric said. "Everyone be on guard."

The sounds of their footsteps echoed off the rocks. Every whisper seemed like a shout.

Suddenly, a voice boomed down from above. "Stop where you are!"

Everyone froze.

Thwomp! A dark, slithering shape leaped down from the rocks and planted itself in the path before them.

The creature was seven feet tall. It had scaly green skin, thick arms and legs, and a long thorny tail. Horns grew on its head.

Its gnarled face had three angry eyes glowing red.

And its mouth sparked and sizzled with fire.

"It's him!" Eric cried. "The dream monster!"

"And the treasure monster!" Khan added.

"But where is his pig nose?" Neal whispered.

"I am Gryndal," the creature shouted. "King of the elves!" His voice boomed as loud and as deep as thunder.

"Elves?" said Neal. "But where are the rosy cheeks? The twinkling eyes? The cute little hat? That's what elves are supposed to look like."

"Give up your treasure or we shall fight you!" Gryndal roared. "Come, my elves!"

A bunch of other creatures jumped from the rocks. But they weren't like Gryndal at all.

There were six of them. They were three feet tall and wore long orange cloaks. Their faces were hidden by huge hoods. Each had a sack over its shoulder and a fistful of long shiny palm leaves. They waved them menacingly.

But they didn't seem very scary.

"Behold my elves! Ruthless and terrible they are!" Gryndal thundered. "Kindly give them all your valuables and no one will be hurt!"

Keeah snorted at that. "We will not! In fact, we have come to take our treasure back!"

"Oh, want to play tough, do you?" Gryndal boomed. "Then take this!"

Blampf! He shot a blast of fire at the kids. Luckily, Keeah sent a bolt of blue lightning in front of the fire. *Ka-whoom!* The fire vanished.

"That won't stop us!" Keeah said. "Attack!"

In a flash, Khan's tough little arms swung into action, but two hooded elves jumped him and began swatting him with their palm leaves.

They grabbed for his canteen, but Khan tossed it high. Eric caught it and tucked it into his belt.

Neal dashed to help Khan, pulling one elf back by his long cloak. "Eat sand, dune boy!" he said.

Then he grabbed at the second elf and managed to pull off his sack before the elf wriggled away. Neal slung the sack over his own shoulder and helped Khan to his feet.

"I got some treasure back!" said Neal.

"Now let's get the thieves, too!" Khan said.

Another elf swatted at Julie, then lunged at Eric, snatching Khan's canteen from his belt.

"Shiny treasure!" the elf squeaked.

"It's a water bottle!" Eric shouted.

"It's shiny!" the elf cried. "Gryndal wants it!"

He pinched Eric's ears and jumped away, dragging his long orange cloak behind him.

"Looks like they bought the wrong size uniform at the bad-guy shop!" Julie said, jumping to her feet. "I'd say they take . . . an extra small!"

Blampf! Gryndal's next fire blast forced Keeah back against the stones. "Give me that harp," he boomed. "Or be a toasted wizard!"

"Oh, you couldn't play it!" Keeah said. "It's not for creepy lizards like you!"

Gryndal stepped back and took a deep breath. Flames sparked from his toothy mouth.

"Back off, chili-breath!" Julie cried. She leaped at Gryndal. Then something heavy hit the ground.

Clank! Julie looked back. The monster was staring at the ground next to her.

There, lying in the dust, was his tail.

It was thrashing this way and that in the sand.

"Whoa!" cried Julie. "I am tougher than I thought! Score one for the kids!"

Suddenly — *poomf! Poomf!*

Loud blasting noises echoed into the pass. The ground thundered. The air grew smoky.

"Someone is coming," cried Gryndal.

He quickly grabbed his tail and leaped clumsily back onto the rocks. "Follow me, elves. Back to the tower."

Instantly, his troops scurried back into the rocks, yipping and yapping.

Poomf! Another puff of gray smoke shot up from the end of the pass.

"What is that?" Neal asked.

"I don't know," said Keeah. "But it saved us!"

Clippity-bang! Rrrrr-ping! Poof-poof!

A strange vehicle rolled between the high rocks and down the path to them.

It looked a little like an old-fashioned car.

And a parade float.

And a steamboat on wagon wheels.

Choof! With a final blast of smoke, the thing jerked to a stop in front of them. A small hatch opened and out popped a strange little man.

He had fuzzy green hair sticking up in little wisps over his long ears. His fingers were delicate. His eyes were thoughtful. He wore a neat brown suit and silver spectacles on his nose.

"Come on up!" he called down in a cheery voice. "My name is Friddle! Sorry to scare you, but I sensed you were in trouble!"

The friends looked at one another. Then they climbed up to the hatch.

"Thanks!" said Eric. "You came just in time."

"Indeed!" said Friddle. "But we must hurry to get there before nightfall."

"Get there?" said Julie as they all took seats inside the strange car's cabin. "Get *where*?"

"Why, to the tower, of course!" said the little man. "The tower of the elf king!"

The kids stared at one another.

"But won't Gryndal be there?" asked Neal.

"Yes," the man replied. "And all of your treasure, too!"

Six

The Story on the Stones

Choof! Choof! Friddle pulled back on the control lever and a great puff of smoke burst from the stack behind them. The whole wagon shook.

"Forward we go!" cried Friddle gleefully. In no time the vehicle was bouncing over the dunes, spraying sand behind it.

"I'm Keeah," said the princess. She introduced everyone. "Why were you in the pass, Friddle?"

The little man grinned. "I've been following Gryndal. Ever since he appeared out of nowhere nearly a moon ago."

Eric glanced at Keeah. "The same time Sparr disappeared."

"Gryndal and his elves robbed my workshop," Friddle added. "I invent things, you know."

Neal laughed. "I love your motorized cart."

"Thank you!" the man said. He opened a slit in front of the cabin. Warm air rushed in.

"I've made quite a study of elves," he went on. "They like to live in the ground. There are twenty-seven varieties, and most of them are quite harmless. But whoever heard of a seven-foot-tall elf with scaly skin and a tail like a swamp lizard?"

Neal raised his hand. "I never did!"

"Ah, so perhaps he is not really a swamp lizard," said Friddle. "One wonders. . . ."

"Well, whatever he is," said Eric, "he's not just stealing jewels, but water bottles, too."

Julie laughed. "Which reminds me, Neal. What's in the sack you managed to steal back?"

"Yes!" said Khan. "Is my crown in there?"

Neal pulled open the sack he had taken from one of the elves. He looked into it.

He slumped his shoulders. "Oh, man!"

"What is it?" Eric stuck his hand into the sack and pulled out a shiny metal object.

Khan sighed. "A spoon?"

"Not just *a* spoon," said Eric. "*Lots* of them!"

Neal tried to grin. "To eat our meatballs with?"

Puff! Chug! Hisss! The cart bounced along, slipping into the dips between the dunes and roaring up out of them again.

Suddenly, there was another sound.

Pling! Thrum! Blong!

"Yes?" said Friddle.

"Sorry," said Keeah. "It's this harp. Sometimes it plays all by itself. I think it's broken."

"Oh, really?" said Friddle. He pushed his spectacles up on his nose and squinted first at the harp, then at the princess. "May I take a look?"

Keeah nodded.

Friddle's long, slender fingers took the harp. A strange smile crept across his face as he studied it. Finally, he set it on his lap and sighed.

"I remember when I made this —"

Keeah nearly fell off her little seat. "You? You made the harp? Then you must be —"

"The Maker?" Friddle quaked with sudden laughter. "Oh, that silly name! Yes, I suppose I deserve it. I make all sorts of things. But then . . . you must be Kee-Kee?"

Keeah beamed. "My mother called me that! She's Queen Relna!"

Friddle laughed brightly. "I'm sorry I didn't recognize you. It was years ago. You've grown into a fine princess!"

"Thank you," said Keeah.

"But the harp, poor thing, has seen better days," said the Maker. "The story stones are all painted over."

"Story stones?" Julie said. "What are they?"

Friddle pulled back one of the levers. The wagon chugged along by itself.

"Magical gems," he said, turning to the children. "They show the story of a person's life. I set twelve blank ones in the queen's harp. We must restore them to their original beauty. And see what story they tell us!"

Friddle took a bottle off a shelf in the cart, opened it, and daubed a cloth with its liquid. It smelled like raspberries, Eric thought.

"What are the harp's powers?" asked Keeah.

Friddle made a low whistling sound as he wiped the harp with the cloth. "That depends on who uses it and how. It can fly, of course, and talk. . . ."

"Talk?" said Keeah.

"Why yes," said Friddle. "When it plinged just now, it called my name. You just have to learn to listen. Ah, there!"

The harp suddenly sparkled with a rainbow of colored stones.

"See here?" he said, pointing to the first stone. "This shows the castle where your mother was born. And here is the cottage your father built for her —"

"That's where I found the harp!" Keeah said.

"Yes, yes," Friddle murmured. "This dark one shows Sparr's fortress, where something terrible happened."

"She was cursed there," Keeah said softly.

"And here . . . hmmm." He stopped.

"What is it?" asked Khan, leaning over.

"A white falcon," Friddle said.

Keeah peered closely at the stone. "That's what my mother became when she was cursed."

"Next to it is a blue dragon," Friddle said. "And next to that is . . . a . . ."

"What?" asked Eric, craning his neck for a better look. "I can't see."

Friddle held the harp up to the light. "It's a ruby. It shows . . . a . . . red . . . tiger."

Keeah gasped. "A red tiger! That must be what she is now!"

The Maker sighed. "But look. Two

stones are missing. When you find them, you will know the next shapes your mother will take!"

As Eric watched her, Keeah began to smile even as her eyes blinked back tears.

"A red tiger," she whispered. "I'll search all of Droon to find her."

Friddle smiled at her. "I daresay you will."

He pushed and pulled the buttons and levers on the control panel. "And . . . there it is!"

Eric squinted through the cabin's opening at a dark shape twisting up from the red dunes.

A giant tower.

"Wow, that's one big tower," Eric said. His knees felt weak just looking at it.

Khan squinted at it. "Is that ugly tower where my treasure is?"

Friddle nodded. "I'm afraid so."

The tower *was* ugly. The outer walls were made of large slabs of metal. And all the way to the top were Ninns — hundreds of them — hammering the slabs sloppily together.

"Don't tell me we're going in there," Neal mumbled softly.

Julie nodded. "We're going in there."

"I asked you not to tell me that!" Neal moaned.

The cart gathered speed as the tower loomed ever closer. Eric and Keeah peered through the slit in front.

"Um . . . just a suggestion," said Eric, "but shouldn't we slow down?"

"Why?" asked Friddle as the cart sped faster.

"Because . . . we're going to crash!" Neal cried.

"Ever hear of crashing a party?" Friddle said. "Gryndal certainly won't invite us in, so hold on to your seats. We're — going — in! Khan, good chap, press that button, would you?"

The Lumpy king pushed a red button on the panel. *Flink-flink!* Two large metal horns popped out of the front of the cart.

They looked like bull's horns.

"What are those for?" Julie asked.

"You'll see!" said Friddle.

The wagon raced over the dunes. Faster and faster and faster it sped, until —

"Holy crow!" Eric yelled. "Hold on!"

Crunch! The horns on the cart pierced straight through the outer wall of the tower!

Ninns with Hammers

Plink! A small door popped open in the front of the wagon. Stale air poured into the cabin.

"I think we're inside," Friddle whispered.

"And still alive!" said Eric as they crawled through the nose of the cart and into the tower.

Friddle remained behind. "I'll draw the Ninns' attention away from you. You'll be safe to search for your treasure. Good luck, my new friends!"

Keeah slung her harp firmly over her shoulder and shook Friddle's small hand. "Thank you for helping us. And thank you for making my harp even more precious to me. We'll see you again soon. That's a promise!"

"I hope to be of service, Princess Kee-Kee!" Friddle pulled his wagon away and turned it. Instantly, a troop of Ninns jumped down from the tower and gave chase as the wagon sped away.

"Quickly now, children," said Khan firmly. "Before we are discovered."

Thwam! Clonk! Thwam! Clonk!

The sounds of iron banging on iron echoed inside the tower. Dozens of red-faced Ninns were gathered around a blazing fire in the center.

"I know the Ninn lady gave you meatballs, Eric," whispered Julie. "But these guys look pretty mean."

Eric nodded. "Yeah. Plus they're working for a very bad dude. We can't forget that."

Some Ninns took giant pieces of iron from the fire and banged them into slabs using huge double-headed hammers.

When the slabs were cool, some other Ninns dragged the pieces up a long, circular stairway.

The kids looked up. The black walls continued up as far as they could see. The stairway circled the inside wall all the way to the top.

"The Ninns haven't seen us yet," said Keeah. "Let's get as far as we can before they do."

"That plan gets my vote," said Neal. "Ninns with hammers are not my favorite thing."

Julie looked around. "First rule of towers: The bad guy always lives at the tippy-top."

"Second rule," said Khan. "That's where he keeps his loot. Now, come on. I can almost smell my crown."

Eric gulped as Julie and Khan jumped into the lead. They slid onto the stairway and climbed up quietly. Neal and Keeah were next, then Eric.

The higher they climbed, the more wobbly the stairs seemed to become.

"I have a question," Eric whispered to Keeah. "Why is an elf king building a tower? Friddle told us that elves like to live in the ground."

Keeah shook her head. "I don't know. But I think we'll find out when we get to the top."

The top. Right. Eric knew they were going there, but he didn't like wobbly stairs. Especially because at every complete turn of the tower, there was an opening to the outside. He could see the ground getting farther and farther away.

"Slow and steady," Eric said. "No sudden movements."

Then the stairs began to shake.

Neal turned. "The Ninns are coming! Look!"

Six Ninns were dragging a slab of iron up the stairs. They hadn't spotted the kids yet, but they were getting closer.

"We can't go down," said Julie. "The Ninns will see us."

Khan looked toward the top. "The Ninns will bring that slab all the way up. We can't hide there, either."

Keeah bit her lip and looked around. Finally, she looked down at the stairs themselves. "We can't be on the stairs when the

Ninns come by. So there's only one thing to do."

"Jump?" asked Eric. "Please don't say that."

Neal laughed. "No, dude. I think what Keeah means is . . . we need to hide *under* the stairs."

"Under?" said Eric. "But how?"

"Everyone, take hold of my harp," Keeah said, holding it out. They did.

"Harp, under the stairs!" she said.

Then the harp — with all five of them clinging tightly to it — floated out beyond the stairs and quickly ducked beneath them.

The children dangled in the shadows. *Stomp! Stomp!* The Ninns were getting closer.

"Oh, I don't like this," said Eric. "Not at all."

The Ninns tramped heavily overhead, scraping and dragging the iron slab upward. They pulled the slab through an arched opening and began to hammer it into place.

Clonk! Clang! Boom!

After what seemed like hours, the Ninns finally trudged back down the stairs to the bottom.

The harp quickly floated the kids back up.

"Um, that was fun," Eric murmured. "Not."

Julie pointed across the open tower to the stairs on the far side. "The steps end at a door. It must lead to Gryndal's hideout."

They took the last few turns together.

"My treasure is near," said Khan.

Keeah put her finger to her lips and pushed open the door. The room inside was bare.

The treasure was not there.

But something else was.

Gryndal. King of the elves.

His ugly, scaly back was to them.

His tail, which appeared to have grown back, was swishing across the floor.

Gryndal stood in the center of the room, gazing out a small round window.

As the kids slid in, Neal's bag of spoons touched the narrow doorway. The bag made the slightest of sounds.

Clink.

It was enough.

Gryndal whirled around. "What!" he shrieked. "You scared me!"

Eric blinked. "We scared . . . *you?*"

King of the Hog Elves

Gryndal tried to blast them with a breath of fire. But — *pooof!* — the force of the blast knocked him backward. He toppled to the floor.

Clonk! His leg fell off. Then one of his arms went flying. His tail crumpled and skittered across the room.

Gryndal tried to get up, but something gave out a loud snapping noise. He toppled again. That made his head — the head with three red eyes and a fire-breathing mouth — fall backward like a helmet off his neck. His chubby pink neck.

Gryndal sighed. "Oh, fumbly-bumbly!"

The kids stared at him.

"Whoa!" Neal gasped. "He's fake!"

"Don't come any closer!" Gryndal snorted.

Khan and Keeah edged over anyway. Neal, Eric, and Julie crept up behind them. They kept staring.

Gryndal was not a monster anymore.

Instead of a scary scaly face, there was a plump pink one. Whiskers stuck out of a thick, flat nose with three nostrils.

His legs and arms were short, and his hair stuck out in wispy patches across his forehead.

He had a curled tail with little bumps all

up and down it. He wore a baggy orange suit.

And he was the size of a turkey.

Khan gasped. "Of the twenty-seven kinds of elves, you must be — a hog elf!"

"Aha!" said Neal. "The pig nose! I knew it!"

Gryndal waddled out of the pile of monster parts. "Very funny, very funny," he snorted.

His voice was snuffly and growly. He wiped his nose on his orange sleeve and looked helplessly up at the kids.

"Oh, let me at him!" Khan growled, but Keeah held him back.

"Why the monster costume?" she asked.

"Ha!" Gryndal snorted. "Do you think the Ninns would obey me? Build a tower for me — a hog elf? Pah! They are scared by glowing eyes and puffs of fire!"

"Uh, so were we," said Julie. "A little."

"A lot," whispered Eric.

"But now," the elf went on, "I no longer need the Ninns. My tower is nearly finished. The treasure is on top. And I shall soon be gone!"

"Gone where?" asked Julie. "Up?"

Gryndal snickered and looked nervously out the window. "Perhaps . . ."

Eric looked out, too. Clouds lay like a fluffy carpet below them. *Below* them.

"Looks like we caught you just in time, then," said Keeah. "We want our treasure."

"Yes!" said Khan. "Give it back right now. My people need it — it belongs to them."

Gryndal looked at them. It seemed as if he was going to speak, then he turned away. "I have a duty to my own people, too. That sorcerer Sparr cursed me and my fellows."

Gryndal paused to look out the window again.

Why does Gryndal keep looking out? Eric wondered. *What's going to happen?*

"It was terrible!" the hog elf went on. "One whole year Sparr kept us cursed in the stone mills of Feshu."

"Sparr is gone," said Julie.

"That's what ended our curse," Gryndal said. "But we found ourselves far from our home of Morka. I need that treasure to fly home."

Keeah frowned. "Fly home? How?"

"The soarwings!" Gryndal said. "Giant birds who live in Morka but circle Droon once a year. They fly above the clouds, only stopping for shiny things. That's why I needed the treasure to get their attention."

Eric glanced around. The room's ceiling stood thirty feet overhead. Above that was the top of the tower. Where the treasure was.

The only way up there was out the window.

They'd have to get up there somehow. Gulp.

Hanging from stairs is one thing, thought Eric. *But climbing up the outside of a tower that's higher than the clouds?*

"I need that treasure!" Gryndal insisted. "Because — look! The soarwings are coming!"

The kids rushed to the window.

Far in the distance were two enormous birds. Their giant, bright-feathered wings flapped slowly as they made their way over the clouds.

It was too much for Khan. He jumped up and down, crying, "Give me my crown!"

"Not till I'm through with it!" the hog elf replied. He put his chubby fingers in his

mouth and puffed. Instead of fire, a sharp whistling noise came out. *Eeeee!*

An instant later, his six fellow elves pounded through the door behind the kids. They swished their palm leaves back and forth.

"I think we're outnumbered," said Neal.

"Come, my elves!" Gryndal announced. "We are going home. And no one shall stop us!"

Suddenly — *blam!* The door burst open again. This time, five Ninn warriors stomped in.

They were red-faced, they were huge, they were mad.

And they weren't wearing dresses!

Nine

The Magic Words

The Ninns looked at Gryndal. Then at the pile of monster parts. Then at Gryndal again.

"You are hog!" one Ninn grunted. "Ugly hog!"

The elf king wiped his nose. "Well, yes. . . ."

"Tower is finished!" said another Ninn.

"Give us treasure now!" grunted a third. "You made promise."

Khan jumped. "You promised *my* treasure to the Ninns?"

Gryndal shuffled to the window. "I had to! I needed my tower built!"

Eric didn't know whether to feel sorry for Gryndal or not. His enemy was Lord Sparr. That put them on the same side. But he stole the Lumpies' treasure, and that was bad.

The Ninns glanced at one another. They grumbled for a while. It seemed like they were deciding what to do next. Then they stopped.

Eric guessed they had made up their minds.

"We get you!" the Ninns shouted.

"Stay away from me!" Gryndal squeaked. "Or I shall roar like . . . like . . . like the red tiger!"

Keeah gasped. She trembled. She screamed, "STOP!"

Everyone did stop. Even the Ninns. They all stared at Keeah. She stepped over to Gryndal.

"Did you say . . . the red tiger?" she asked.

Gryndal slid closer to the window. "The red tiger. Yes, I saw her. They say she was a queen cursed by Sparr. I know where she is."

"She is my mother!" Keeah shouted. "Tell me what you know! Tell me everything!"

The elf king looked out the window. The birds were flying closer. "Well, I would, but you see — I must go. I must go — now!"

In a flash, Gryndal climbed out the window.

"Wait!" Keeah cried. She bolted out after him.

The six hog elves followed her.

"I guess it's our turn," said Julie. "Come on!"

But the Ninns came back to themselves. They blinked and growled and got mad again.

"Get children," they shouted. "They help Gryndal! They are enemies of Lord Sparr!"

The red-faced warriors drew their swords.

"Oh! Big swords!" Khan said. "Very big!"

"Get back, you dudes!" said Neal, stepping accidentally into Eric. The two boys stumbled and hit the floor together.

Clang-a-lang! Splat! Their bags full of meatballs and spoons spilled out next to them.

The Ninns waved their swords.

Eric looked at Neal and grinned. "Are you thinking what I'm thinking?" he asked.

Neal smiled back. "Don't hog the food! Everybody — grab a spoon!"

As the Ninns edged closer, the kids all grabbed spoons. They loaded meatballs onto the spoons. Then they pulled back on the spoons . . . and let go!

Fwing! Splat! Plop! Slurp!

The room was a storm of flying meat-balls!

"Eek! Aff! Oop!" The Ninns scattered under the rain of meatballs. They shielded their heads. They crouched low. They ran for cover.

Then the meatballs ran out.

"Uh-oh," Julie mumbled. "Out of ammo."

The Ninns made gargling noises. Eric knew what this meant. The Ninns were laughing.

They started after the kids again.

Then Eric remembered something. It

was what the Ninn woman had said in the tent. He wasn't sure if it would work, but he said it anyway. Loudly.

"Thalak!" he yelled.

The Ninns jerked to a stop. They looked at one another, then at Eric, grumbled, stepped back, then tramped out the door and down the stairs.

Neal stared at Eric. "Dude, that was awesome!" He slapped Eric's hand in a low-five.

"Nice choice of words," said Julie. "What does *thalak* mean?"

Eric shrugged. "We'll find out later. Right now, we need to help Keeah!"

He jumped to the window. He peered out and up. The rough surface of the tower jutted above him. The hog elves were escaping up the side.

He gulped. He didn't want to follow them.

But he had to.

Here goes! he said to himself. Eric pulled himself out the window. He clung to the side and began to climb.

"Slow and steady," he murmured. "No sudden movements."

Then there came the terrifying sounds of iron being ripped apart. The tower shuddered.

"Oh, man!" Eric cried. "Please . . . no!"

"The Ninns are shaking the tower!" Khan said, climbing out the window below Eric.

"They're hopping mad," said Julie. "They're tearing the tower apart!"

Neal scrambled up behind them. "Not even spoons will save us now — we're doomed!"

Ten

A Wizard's Journey

Eric's knees felt weak. His stomach fluttered. But he kept climbing, hand over hand, up the side of the tower.

Then, suddenly, there they were. Two enormous silver birds swooping down from the sky.

The air hummed as the soarwings circled the tower. Sunlight glinted off their feathers in a rainbow of colors.

At last, Eric tugged himself to the tower's top.

Standing before him was a huge mound of shimmering gold and jeweled objects.

Khan's treasure.

Keeah tried to rush to Gryndal, but his elves jumped in the way, swishing their palm leaves.

The tower shuddered again. It began to swing back and forth.

"Come here, soarwings!" Gryndal cried out.

Fwap! Fwap! The giant birds descended to the treasure, landing on the tower. They made cooing and purring sounds as they picked and rummaged through it with their long beaks.

In a flash, Gryndal leaped onto the feathery back of one of the giant birds.

His six fellow elves jumped on after him.

"Where did you see my mother?" Keeah demanded. "Tell me where!"

"Beyond the rocky coast of Mintar, near the Bangledorn Forest," Gryndal shouted. "That is where I was cursed. That is where I saw your mother —"

Fwap! Fwap! Gryndal's bird began to rise from the tower. The second bird rose with it. They both pulled away from the tower and circled it once.

"Take your treasure!" Gryndal said, grinning, as he and his men swung the giant bird around. "Take it all! We need it no longer!"

"We are free!" his elves yipped happily. "We are going home!"

Keeah stood there as the tower groaned and twisted with each swing in the air.

Then, in a single swift move, Keeah unslung her harp. She held it before her. And she spoke.

"Harp! Take me up!"

"Keeah!" Eric yelled over the sound of roaring wings. "What are you doing?"

But the harp followed her command instantly. In a whoosh of air, Keeah rose from the tower and swept toward the second bird.

"Keeah!" Eric yelled. "Come back! It's too dangerous! We'll go with you!"

The princess flew up to the bird and leaped onto its back. She gripped the neck feathers and the bird circled the tower once more.

Julie and Neal finally clambered over the top. Khan rushed to the treasure heap and stopped.

They all looked up.

Keeah's eyes sought out her friends' faces one by one. "We finally have the treasure," she cried. "But now I must go. Gryndal knows more than he is telling. I must find out!"

She turned, smiled bravely at Eric, and waved.

"Keeah!" Eric called. "Wait!"

But she rode the giant bird over the clouds toward the sun.

"Eric, we better get out of here," Julie said. "This tower —"

Crrrrk! A chunk of the tower cracked away and fell to the ground. Another huge piece split off and tumbled down.

The tower began to split.

"Uh-oh," said Neal. "I think we've stayed too long at Gryndal's party!"

Khan found his crown and plunked it on his head. "Yes!" he cried. "My people have their treasure back! Now come. We must hurry!" He began to stuff a sack with his treasure.

"Too bad we didn't think of parachutes!" Neal said, helping Khan stuff his sack. "Did anybody think about how we're going to get down?"

Eric gulped. He looked around. "Um, no . . ."

Suddenly — *fwoosh!* — flames rushed up the side of the tower. A bright blue shape floated by.

"Oh, man! Now what?" Julie cried.

"Jump aboard!" yelled a voice.

Eric peered through the clouds. "Friddle?"

"The one and only!" the little man chirped. He was standing in the basket of a giant hot-air balloon. "Come aboard! The tower is breaking up!"

In a flash, Julie and Neal jumped into the basket. Then Khan swung his giant bag of treasure aboard and leaped in himself.

"Whooooa!" Eric took a running jump just as the tower wobbled again. He had barely reached the basket when the tower swung one last time.

But this time, it didn't swing back.

The Ninns cheered as the tower of the elf king crashed to the dunes below. *Ka-whoom!*

A moment later, all was quiet.

As the balloon floated gently lower, Eric felt sad and happy at the same time. Keeah was following her dream. With every mile, she was getting closer. But weren't they also losing a friend?

"I wish we could help her," he said.

The Maker turned to him. "And with all our hearts, we shall!" His eyes twinkled as he spoke.

"We'll help her with all the magic Droon can muster," Khan said.

"And inventions," said Friddle happily.

"And teamwork," said Julie.

The two soarwings were now only tiny dots on the horizon. The purple dawn turned golden.

"Keeah's dream calls her," Friddle said. "Yours will call you back here soon. And you will see her again. Your lives are bound to hers. That, I can tell."

Eric looked deeply into the strange little man's eyes. He liked what he saw there.

He liked what Friddle had said, too.

It sounded good. It sounded right.

"The stairs," said Khan. "I see them."

The staircase shimmered brightly atop a high dune. Friddle landed the balloon nearby. Everyone got out.

Khan, with his crown perched firmly on his head, was his cheery old self again. Over his back he slung his enormous sack of treasure.

"Things will be happy again in Lumpland," he said to the children. "Thank you for your help."

"Wait a second," said Neal. "We never did learn what *thalak* means."

Eric turned to Friddle. "I said it to the Ninns and they went away. What does it mean?"

The small man scratched his chin, then roared with laughter. "Roughly, it means — 'I'll pinch your cheeks if you don't go away!' Yes, Eric, I am sure you confused those poor Ninns!"

With that, Eric and his friends raced up the stairs. At the top, they watched the giant birds rise higher and higher into the brightening sky.

Neal flicked on the light.

Whoosh! The floor appeared. Droon was gone.

For now.

"That was one awesome adventure,"

said Julie. "It seems strange that Keeah is just . . . gone."

"We'll find her," said Eric firmly.

"You better believe it," said Neal. Then he added, "So . . . anyone for chili dogs?"

Eric looked at his friends. He couldn't help but smile. "Gotta eat, I guess. To keep in shape for our next adventure!"

Julie started for the basement stairs. "How about . . . last one in the pool is a . . ."

"Hog elf!" Neal yelled. "Snort, snort!"

Laughing together, the three friends charged up the stairs and outside to join the party.

Quest for
the Queen

To Benjamin McCormack,
a good friend, faithful reader,
and wizard in the making

One

A New Kind of Homework

Rub! Scrub! Splash!

Eric Hinkle bent over the sink in the bathroom at school. He swished his hands in the soapy water, trying to clean up after gym.

"You're lousy at climbing ropes," he said to his friend Neal. "Did you have to fall on me?"

"I'm better at watching things than doing them," Neal said as he scrubbed dirt from his shirt, his nose, and his shoes. "I think it's a sign of smartness."

"That's not what the coach said," said Eric. Then he sighed. "Man, we need to go back."

"To class?" said Neal. "Mrs. Michaels promised us a math quiz. Can't we be a little late?"

Eric turned to face him. "No, I mean to Droon! I can't think about anything else."

It was true. Droon was always on Eric's mind.

It had all begun one day when he and Neal and their friend Julie were cleaning up his basement. Well, they were *supposed* to be cleaning up. Mostly they were playing around.

Then, behind some boxes, they had discovered a small closet. Inside the closet was a rainbow-colored staircase. It led to another world.

A magical world called Droon.

Neal splashed water on his nose. "I know what you mean. It's kind of boring here. Julie wants to go back, too. I just hope Keeah is okay."

Keeah was one of the first people the kids had met in Droon. She was a young princess learning to be a junior wizard. An old and very powerful wizard named Galen Longbeard was teaching her all the magic she needed to know.

But what Keeah wanted to know most was when her mother would be free of an evil spell.

For years, Keeah's mother, Queen Relna, had been changing into one animal after another. She had to go through many shapes until she could be human again.

At the end of their last adventure, Keeah had learned that the queen was now in the form of a red tiger.

To find her, Keeah had flown away on the back of a giant bird. The kids didn't know what had happened next.

"I wish we could go back whenever we want," said Eric. "I don't like waiting."

Usually, the kids dreamed about Droon. Sometimes Keeah sent them a message through an enchanted soccer ball. But until one of those things happened, Eric and his friends just had to wait.

Tap! Tap! There was a knock at the lavatory door. "Guys?"

It was Julie's voice. "Mrs. Michaels wants you back right now," she said. "It's quiz time."

Neal looked at his shirt in the mirror. It was soaking wet. "Well, my work here is done. See you in class." He left Eric alone at the sink.

Eric was about to drain the water when he glanced down. The soapsuds swirling in the sink suddenly stopped . . . in the shape of a face.

A sad old face. With a long white beard.

"Galen?" Eric mumbled to himself. "Galen!"

A moment later, the face in the sink was gone.

The water was just water.

Eric dashed back to class and slid into his seat between Julie and Neal. "I just saw Galen floating in the bathroom sink!" he whispered.

"How did he fit in there?" Julie asked.

"No! I mean, his face was in the soap!"

"Eric," said Mrs. Michaels, giving him a stern look. "We'll start our math quiz now." She passed out the papers and stood in front of the room. "You will have ten minutes to finish. Starting . . . now."

Eric looked at the paper but all he could think about was the wizard's face.

Why had Galen appeared to him? Why had he looked so sad? Was something wrong?

Eric felt a tug on his sleeve. It was Julie. She was staring at the chalkboard.

He looked up. He nearly fell out of his seat.

A piece of yellow chalk was floating up behind the teacher's back. Silently, it pressed against the green board and began to write.

Eric glanced around. Everyone else was busy working on the quiz. Their heads were down.

The chalk began to spell out letters.

S . . . h . . . e . . .

Eric slid his foot out and tapped Neal's sneaker. Neal looked up. His mouth dropped open.

. . . i . . . s . . .

The chalk hesitated as Mrs. Michaels

glanced at the clock. "Five more minutes," she said.

The chalk continued writing.

. . . l . . . o . . . s . . . t . . .

She is lost. Eric's eyes widened. *She?* *Keeah!*

Mrs. Michaels started to turn around.

Then the eraser flashed up from the bottom of the board and — *swish!* — wiped away what the chalk had written. Eric and his friends were the only ones to see the message.

They were the only ones *meant* to see it.

They were so excited they could hardly finish the quiz. When the final bell rang, they burst from the classroom and rushed out to their bus.

"Galen must have sent the message!" Eric whispered. "I think it's about Keeah."

Julie nodded. "She must have gotten

lost trying to find her mother. And now we need to find her!"

"It's like homework," said Neal. "Only from Droon!"

Ten minutes later, the bus stopped at their corner. They raced into Eric's house and were down in his basement in no time.

Neal and Julie pulled aside some heavy boxes. Behind the boxes was the door to a small closet nestled under the basement steps.

The kids piled into the closet and shut the door behind them. Eric looked at Julie and Neal.

"Everybody ready?" he asked.

They nodded.

Julie turned off the light. *Click*.

For an instant, the small room was dark. Then — *whoosh!* — the floor vanished beneath them, and they stood at the top of a long, shimmering staircase.

They never knew where the stairs would lead, only that one of their Droon friends would meet them at the bottom.

A warm wind blew as the three friends began to descend the stairs.

The sky around them was glowing pink.

"There's a coastline below," said Julie. "Some sand. Lots of sharp rocks. There's a big sea on one side and a forest on the other. It looks okay."

"I don't see anybody down there," said Neal. "Where's our welcome committee?"

"Let's just be careful," said Eric cautiously. "We can't be sure of anything."

That was true. There were lots of friendly creatures and people in Droon, but there were other types, too.

An evil sorcerer named Lord Sparr had long been trying to take over Droon. He was in hiding now, but the kids knew he could pop up at any moment.

As Eric looked out across the crashing waves, he also remembered the mysterious witch named Demither, who ruled under the sea.

The last time they saw her, Demither had transformed herself into a giant sea serpent.

Ka-splursh! Waves splashed over the rocks below.

"I see a boat!" said Julie, pointing to a small shape bobbing on the waters. "I bet it's Galen coming to welcome us."

"Yes, a friendly face," said Neal. "Let's hurry down and meet him."

They dropped onto the beach just as the staircase faded. They knew it would appear again when it was time to go home.

The boat headed toward them.

"He's trying to land," said Neal.

Ka-whoom! The sea thundered loudly, and a large wave rose up like a hand.

It seemed to grab the tiny boat and hurl it right at the shore.

Right at the jagged rocks.

"Oh, no! Galen's going to hit the rocks! He's going to crash!"

Two

Strange Strangers

Splurshhhh . . .

But the little boat didn't hit the rocks.

It slid neatly between them and up onto the sand. Then it stopped.

"Whoa," said Julie. "That was lucky."

"Or magical," said Eric with a smile. "Good thing for Galen that he knows so many spells."

The three friends ran over to the boat.

It was a small wooden craft with a short mast.

"Hello!" Neal called out. "Anybody at home? I mean . . . at boat!"

The boat jerked once, then — *flonk! whiz! blap!* — its wooden sides flapped down, a set of four wheels popped out from beneath it, the mast collapsed, and a seat flipped over on the front. In seconds, the boat was no longer a boat.

"It looks like a circus wagon," said Neal. "I love circuses!"

"Do you really think it's Galen's?" Julie asked.

Plonk! One last panel slid down into place.

"Not unless he changed his name," said Eric.

The wagon now bore a brightly painted sign:

Tarok the Clown!
Featuring Slag, Mightiest
Man in Droon!

"I love clowns!" said Neal.

Moments later, a door opened on the front of the wagon. Out popped a little man in a big coat. He had a funny horn stuck in his belt, his hair was blue, and his nose was big, red, and false.

He was mumbling quietly to himself but stopped when he saw the children.

Julie stepped forward. "Um . . . hello," she said. "We're glad you didn't crash —"

Honka-honka! The man squeezed his horn suddenly.

"I am Tarok the clown!" he blurted out. "I make millions laugh with my jokes. Here's one! What's the difference between children and fish? Give up? I *like* fish! Ha-ha!"

Eric and his friends looked at one another.

"Does he mean he doesn't like *us*?" Neal whispered.

Tarok jumped up on his seat and waved his arms. "Behold Slag, the Mightiest Man in Droon! Slag? Where are you? SLAG!"

Blam! The back of the wagon flew open and out stepped a large man. A very large man.

Slag was at least seven feet tall.

He had a head as large as a pumpkin and he seemed to be made entirely of muscles.

Julie nudged Eric. "He's bigger than the wagon!" she whispered. "How in the world did he fit in there?"

Slag grinned as he flexed his muscles. His smile showed many teeth missing.

"We're going to the Droon Quest!" said Slag. "In Bangledorn Forest!" He pointed at the wall of trees nearby. "That's the forest."

"Thanks," said Eric. "That's good to know. But what's a Droon Quest?"

Tarok narrowed his beady eyes at them. "The Quest is a great race for a wonderful prize. Everyone's coming from miles around to compete. And I'll be there, making them laugh. My partner, Slag, will perform feats of amazing strength. But right now, we're late. Slag, let's go!"

The giant then reached into the back of the wagon and pulled out a large colorful net made of thick rope. He tossed it over his shoulder.

Then he tugged on something else.

Hrrr! A large shaggy six-legged beast called a pilka clopped out of the wagon.

"Whoa!" said Julie, edging around to the back of the wagon. "What else is in there?"

Blam! Slag slammed the door before she could see inside. Then he hitched the pilka to the wagon, clambered into the seat next to Tarok, and set the net beside him.

"Can I ask what the net is for?" asked Neal.

"We're going fishing, of course!" said Tarok.

Julie blinked. "But you're heading to the forest. How can you fish in a forest?"

"That's the joke!" Tarok said without smiling. "See how funny I am?"

He squeezed his horn once more — *honka-honka!* — then snapped the reins. The yellow wagon sped quickly across the beach.

Eric waited for it to disappear into the forest before he spoke. "Were those guys weird or were they weird?"

"Both," muttered Julie. "And a little scary, too. But besides that, if Galen did call us here, why didn't he meet us at the stairs?"

"Do you think maybe he's at this Droon Quest thing?" asked Neal.

Eric scanned the forest. "Maybe. At least now we know that this is Bangledorn Forest. It's ruled by a queen named Ortha, I think."

"Right," said Julie. "And Ortha is friends with Keeah. Maybe she can help us find her."

"Finally," Neal added. "After the unfunniest clown and the hugest muscle man in Droon, it'll be good to find some real friends. Let's get moving."

Bangledorn Forest was like a jungle — enormous, dark, and hot. Brightly colored birds began crowing the moment the kids entered.

"Caww! Keee! Rooo-woo!"

Leaves fluttered and hanging vines

twitched above them as they searched for a path.

"It's kind of spooky in here," said Eric.

"Don't worry," said Julie. "This seems pretty much like a rain forest. We studied one in science, remember? We'll be okay. Just stay cool."

"Stay cool?" said Neal, flapping his shirt. "It's a rain forest. It must be a hundred degrees —"

Crack! There was a loud noise in the bushes.

"Run!" said Eric. But they couldn't run.

Something large and swift came crashing through the trees and leaped onto the path in front of them.

Neal jumped. "Holy cow, I mean — *tiger*!"

It was a tiger.

A tiger covered with red fur.

Rowww! It growled loudly, but there was something strange in the sound. At once, the kids knew. This wasn't just any tiger.

"My gosh!" cried Julie. "Could it be? I think it's . . . it's . . . Queen Relna!"

As if it understood Julie's words, the animal slowed. Its red fur rippled from head to tail.

Its black eyes started in fear.

Then the tiger spoke. "My young friends, find Keeah. Tell her the hour has come for me to change, but there is danger. I am being followed. Tell her . . . beware . . . the . . . magic!"

Then, as swiftly as it had appeared, the tiger jumped away through the trees.

"Queen Relna!" Julie yelled. "Wait! Don't go!"

But the red tiger was gone.

Eric stared around into the thick woods. "I don't see anything following her. She sure looked frightened, though."

"You can add me to that list," said Neal. "Man, I wish Keeah were here . . . Whooooa!"

Suddenly, Neal leaped ten feet in the air, twirled once, then shot straight up into a tree.

Julie gaped at him. "How did you do that?"

"I didn't!" Neal cried. "Something *threw* me up here!"

The next thing Eric knew, his feet were yanked out from under him and — "Yikes!" — he, too, was hurled into the tree.

Julie looked at them. "Well, of all the — hey!"

Now she was jerked up from the ground, swung around like a propeller,

and — *fwing!* — thrown into the tree with Neal and Eric.

"Who *did* that?" she howled.

The only answer was a sound — *thumpa! thumpa!* — as heavy footsteps crashed after the tiger and away into the woods.

Three

The Wonder in the Trees

"Can somebody help me down?" said Neal, doubled over a thick branch. "I can't move."

"My foot is stuck," Eric moaned. "Someone has to unstick me. . . ."

"Stop complaining," snapped Julie, trying to get her arms free. "Help me instead!"

"Shhh!" Neal hissed. "Somebody's coming!"

The kids looked down.

Trotting up the path was a spry old man. He wore a ragged cloak with a hood, thick glasses, and a long, droopy mustache.

"Hey, sir!" Julie called out to the man. "Can you help us down from this tree?"

The old man stopped under the tree and blinked up through his glasses at the kids. "Oh, my gosh! It's you!"

Krrripp! The stranger tugged off the mustache, tore off the glasses, and shook off the old clothes.

Julie squealed when she saw who it was. "Keeah! It's Keeah! It's her! It's you!"

It was Princess Keeah.

"I'm so glad you're here!" she said brightly.

Keeah's crown shone in her long blond hair. On her back she carried her mother's magic harp.

"How did you know to come to Droon?" she asked as she quickly climbed the tree and helped her friends down one by one.

"Galen was in the sink at school!" said Eric, rubbing his ankle. "Well, his face was."

"Then the chalk wrote *She is lost* on the board," Neal added. "We figured Galen meant that you were lost."

"Me? Lost?" Keeah said, her eyes widening.

"The last time we saw you, you flew away on a big bird," said Julie. "We were worried. I guess Galen was, too."

"Oh, no," said Keeah. "I've been in disguise searching for my mother. Now everyone thinks I'm lost —"

"Plus, we saw your mom," said Neal. "She said she needs to change shapes, but somebody's following her. She also said, 'Beware the magic.'"

Keeah held up her hand. "Wait." She

closed her eyes for a moment. Then she sighed. "No. She is no longer nearby. Come on. We'd better get to Bangledorn City right away. We need to tell everyone we're safe. This way!"

The princess pushed some leaves aside and jumped onto a narrow path through the trees.

As the kids followed, they told Keeah about Tarok and Slag and the attack in the woods.

Keeah listened carefully. "After I left you, I tracked my mother here to the forest. I went in disguise when I realized someone was hunting for her."

"Can your harp help you find her?" asked Eric. Keeah's magic harp used to belong to her mother. No one knew all the harp's powers, but it had helped the kids many times before.

Keeah held up the small, bow-shaped

instrument and touched a row of colorful gems called story stones. They showed events in Queen Relna's life. One of the stones took the form of a red tiger. The next two stones were missing.

"My harp won't help me here," said Keeah. "No magic is allowed in Bangledorn Forest. Long ago, the forest was proclaimed a place of peace. It's an ancient law of Droon."

Julie frowned. "Sounds like somebody isn't playing by the rules."

"Yeah, the invisible dude," said Neal, rubbing his sore arms. "Met him. Didn't like him."

The princess entered a thick hedge of bushes, then stopped and smiled.

"Even though the laws of Droon do not permit magic here," she said, "amazing things can still happen. If you know where to look."

She pushed through a wall of bright flowering bushes. "Behold . . . Bangledorn City!"

The kids looked around them.

"Holy cow!" said Neal. "It's like the ultimate tree house, except — it's a tree city!"

It was true.

Spreading far up into the distance was a city built of tree houses of all sizes. The houses were made from branches and their roofs were thatched with fat green leaves.

Giant towers were carved into massive tree trunks. They loomed like friendly old men watching over the city. Bridges made of woven vines dangled from one tall tree to the next.

Some of the tallest houses even poked through the very top of the forest.

"This is so amazing!" Eric exclaimed.

"It is one of the great wonders of

Droon," said Keeah, her eyes beaming. "Let's go in."

Boom-thum! Boom-thum! Drums pounded as soon as the children entered the city.

At once, a troop of furry green monkeys scampered down from the trees and surrounded the visitors. "Keeah!" they cried. "Keeah is found!"

Another group of monkeys appeared from nowhere. With them was a tall old man wearing a long blue robe and a tall wizard's hat.

"Galen!" said Keeah, rushing to him.

The wizard hugged the princess as if she were his own daughter. "Ah, my dear Keeah. I searched for you, then lost you in the forest. Even I am not allowed to use my powers here."

He turned to Eric, Neal, and Julie. "Forgive me for not meeting you at the stairs. I

was called to the city. I'm glad you found Keeah so quickly."

Julie laughed. "Well, Keeah sort of found us."

"Yeah, up a tree!" added Neal. "Some kind of invisible dude tossed us up there."

"Invisible?" said Galen with a quick look at Keeah. "So, there is magic here. . . ."

"Keeah! Children!" a happy voice chirped.

It was Max, an eight-legged spider troll with big eyes and orange hair. He scampered down from a tree and hugged Keeah as Galen had.

"You're all here just in time," Max said. "Eric, Julie, Neal, the Droon Quest is today. It happens only once every seven years. It's a great contest of skill and endurance. And also of fun!"

"Cool. Fun is my best sport!" said Neal.

Galen turned to a flight of log stairs ascending to a palace in the trees. "The Quest will begin soon. And for that we must see Ortha, leader of the Bangledorn monkeys. But first, tell me what you have seen. Or, in the case of this invisible person, what you have *not* seen!"

On their way to the palace, Eric, Julie, and Neal told Galen about Tarok and Slag, the invisible attacker, and the red tiger.

"Queen Relna told us, 'Beware the magic,'" Eric added. "We don't know what that means."

Galen paused on the stairs to Ortha's palace. "It means someone is defying the ancient laws of Droon. Upsetting the peace that graces this wonderful forest."

"Who would do that?" asked Julie.

"Only a sorcerer or wizard could," Galen replied. "Since Lord Sparr is in hiding, I can only guess who is behind this unlawful use of magic."

Keeah looked at her friends, then at Galen. "Who *is* behind it?"

Galen's eyes narrowed as he spoke the name. "Witch Demither."

Eric shuddered. They all did.

Galen went on. "As you know, Demither's powers for evil are second only to those of Lord Sparr himself. But what she wants is far from clear. Seven years ago Demither appeared at the last Quest, and she and the queen fought. Oh, a bitter sight it was."

"Who won?" asked Neal. "I'll bet it was the queen."

"No one wins such a conflict," Galen said sharply. "A battle of angry words ending in silence. Demither demanded something. The queen refused. I never learned what it was about. But it was clear to me that the witch held some secret power over Keeah's mother."

"Demither is bad to the core," said Max, snarling. "I do not trust her an inch!"

They stood before the doors of Ortha's palace. Then Galen turned to look out over the forest. The black sea churned angrily in the distance.

"If indeed there is dark magic in the wood today," the wizard said, "then clearly we must be watchful. We must be careful. All of us."

Bong! A deep gonging sound boomed over the trees.

And the great wooden doors of the palace swung open.

Four

Into the Arena

The giant doors parted and out strode Ortha, ruler of the Bangledorn monkeys.

She was tall and slender and her green fur glistened in the sunlight. She wore a long blue cape and a crown made of sharp purple leaves.

She smiled warmly at the kids.

"Welcome, all of you, to our forest," she said. "Keeah, children, I am glad you are safe. You have arrived just in time. The

Quest begins this afternoon. Let me show you . . ."

They entered a giant green room. The leafy ceiling was held aloft by massive wooden pillars.

"This is so cool," Neal said. "It's like being outside . . . inside!"

The sunlight and warm breezy air flowed through the open sides of the palace, fluttering the leaves.

Wood chimes clattered gently from the ceiling.

"It's so magical here," said Julie.

"We Bangledorns live entirely without magic," Ortha said as she swept through the hall. "That is why Queen Relna chose our forest as the site of the Droon Quest. Everyone, no matter who they are, has a chance to win."

Galen turned to Ortha. "Alas, Keeah and the children have seen magic in the woods today. Queen Relna is nearby, but she is not safe. An unknown creature is following her invisibly."

Ortha drew in her breath sharply. "Our forest was never meant to be the battleground of evil forces. But we cannot delay the Quest."

They passed from the room and out onto a balcony overlooking the vast forest.

Below the palace, on the forest floor, was a large open arena. In the center was a field. A great throng of people and strange creatures from every corner of Droon were gathering there. Banners waved, and flags of all sizes and colors flapped over the tents and incoming wagons.

Julie pointed to a long winding path through the forest below. "What's that?" she asked.

"That is the course for the Quest," Ortha said. "Each team races in chariots. The

course twists and turns like a snake and ends at the sea."

"It looks so cool," said Neal. "Can we race?"

The Bangledorn ruler nodded. "Yes, but as with all true quests, it will not be easy. You must race once around the arena, then enter the forest. There you will find obstacles."

"What kind of obstacles?" asked Eric.

"First the walls of fire!" said Max, his eyes growing large. "Then an angry raging river!"

"After that you must race on foot," said Ortha. "Across the beach and across a bridge. "

"A bridge to where?" asked Julie.

"Ah, this is the most wonderful part," said Galen. "On this very day every seven years, an island appears offshore at sundown. When Relna founded the Quest, she chose the island as the place where the Quest would end. It is on the island that the winner will find the prize."

"But you must be quick!" said Max. "The island appears for only a few moments before it vanishes again — for another seven years!"

"Another secret of Droon," Julie said. "Neat!"

"But what is the prize?" asked Eric. "A gold medal? A trophy? Treasure?"

Galen shook his head. "Many legends have grown up about the prize. But it is something worth far more than gold or jewels. For the one meant to win, the prize is what he or she wants most. For all others, it is worthless. The Quest prize is the only magic allowed here."

"Could the prize be a cure for my mother?" Keeah asked breathlessly.

"It could indeed," said Ortha. "Your

mother hoped that someday you would win the prize. It is not only a great honor, but a test of a truly special person."

Keeah looked at the gathering crowd. Then she unslung her harp. "I will try my best." She handed the harp to Galen. "I guess I won't be needing this."

The gong sounded again, and Ortha smiled at the children. "It is time to enter the arena!"

The children, with Max and Keeah leading the way, descended into the Quest arena.

There were all kinds of games and sporting events being held before the big Quest.

One purple Lumpy in a yellow warm-up suit was tossing a large leather ball at a stone wall.

"Okay," said Neal. "The catapult contest."

Nearby a pair of slithery creatures with tiny heads raced into the trees as crowds cheered.

Beyond that, a handful of green monkeys leaped onto vines and swung to see how far they could go before jumping off into a small pond.

Julie grinned. "I love it! It's like the Olympics in our world. I want to be in a race."

"Look!" Max shouted. "The chariots!"

Eric whistled when he saw them. "Oh, cool!"

Before them stood a giant parking lot full of chariots, ready for the Quest.

Each chariot was like a fancy open cart hitched to a single pilka. Some had wings flying up from the back. Others had double sets of wheels. Some had seats, others you stood up in.

But all of them looked very fast.

Keeah hopped into a sleek purple one. "This is the one I'm choosing," she said excitedly. "I love the wings in the back. Besides, it's big enough for four. Would you like to race along with me?"

Julie jumped up and down. "Yes, yes, yes! I'd love to!"

"You bet," said Neal. "Vrrrm-vrrrrrm!"

Eric glanced around at the crowd. "But let's not forget our homework. Galen said to be watchful. If there's magic here, it means someone is disobeying the law."

"I'll watch out for cheaters," said Neal. "But I'm running if I see someone invisible!"

"How can you *see* someone who's invisible?" asked Julie.

Keeah laughed, then stopped suddenly and looked around. "You sense them. . . ."

Eric turned to her. "Are you saying you sense something now?"

Before Keeah could answer, a loud voice yelled behind them. "Out of the way, please!"

A yellow wagon rumbled into the field.

It was Tarok! He seemed to stare at Keeah as he drove his wagon into the arena.

"Tarok the clown is here!" he bellowed. "My show begins in half an hour. You'll laugh so hard . . . you'll cry!"

Julie pulled Keeah close. "That's him!" she whispered as the wagon rolled by. "Tarok is the strange man we told you about."

Keeah watched the yellow wagon rumble away. "It's odd. I feel something, but I'm not sure what —"

"Keeah," said Max, pulling her by the hand. "The vine trials! Everyone's asking for you!"

Keeah took one last look at Tarok's

wagon, then turned and smiled at the kids. "I've always wanted to compete in the high vines event. I'll meet you back here right away. . . ."

"We'll stay here and snoop around," said Eric as Max led Keeah into the crowd.

Julie glanced at Eric and Neal. "What was that all about? Do you think Keeah really sensed something? Maybe magic in the air?"

"It's kind of odd that Tarok should come along just when she felt something," Neal said.

"Maybe not so odd," said Eric, gazing after Tarok. "There's something strange about that clown. I don't trust him, or Slag, either."

"Where is Slag, anyway?" Julie asked.

Neal glanced around the crowd. "You can't miss that guy. Even his muscles have muscles!"

"Both of those dudes give me the major creeps," Julie added.

Eric gave a quick nod. "I'd like to see what else Tarok has in that wagon of his. What do you say we do some serious spying?"

"That gets my vote," said Neal. They all started after Tarok's wagon.

Suddenly, a cry rang out over the arena.

"Help! Princess Keeah's in trouble!"

Five

A Princess in Trouble!

The kids rushed through the crowd. Everyone was staring up into the tall trees at the top of the forest.

Keeah stood on a single slim vine that hung between two trees like a high wire.

But something was wrong.

The vine she was on was rippling and quivering under her as if someone were shaking it.

Eric looked over at the far tree. "Some-one's pulling on Keeah's vine. She'll fall."

"But . . . there's no one there!" said Julie.

"It must be Mr. Invisible!" Neal added. "Tossing people around wasn't bad enough. Now he's messing with our princess!"

In a flash, the kids jumped into action. They started climbing a rope ladder to the top of the first tree.

"Hang in there, Keeah!" Neal yelled up.

"Faster!" said Eric, keeping his eye on the princess as he climbed. "She won't be able to stay on much longer."

They reached a small wooden platform at the top of the tree. It looked as if the vine Keeah was standing on was being wobbled sharply from the platform on the far tree. She was desperately trying to keep her balance.

"What do we do now?" Julie asked.

Eric looked around. Hanging vines dangled all around them. "We do what they do in circuses all the time."

"Juggle?" asked Neal.

"No, like on the trapeze," said Eric. He grabbed one of the vines and tugged on it. "This should hold me," he said.

"Are you nuts?" said Neal. "You fell off the ropes in gym today!"

Eric gave Neal a look. "I fell off because you fell on me! Besides, do you have another idea? Keeah can't use magic. She's like us now. She needs help." He paused. "From people who know what they're doing."

"Okay, okay, don't rub it in," said Neal. "Julie and I will hold the vine tight to make sure it doesn't break. You go and try to reach her. When you do —"

"We'll haul you both in," said Julie. "Simple teamwork. But please be careful."

Eric tied the end of the vine tightly around his waist. He took a deep breath. "Wish me luck."

"Luck," said Neal. "And hurry!"

Eric hoped he could do it. He wasn't very good with ropes. Not as bad as Neal, but still not very good. Still, he had to try.

As soon as he stepped out, the vine strung between the trees shook some more.

"Ohhh!" the crowd gasped.

Eric's heart was racing a mile a minute. He could hardly breathe. He felt hot and cold at the same time. "If this doesn't work . . ." he whispered to himself.

"Never mind! It will work! It has to!"

Neal and Julie tried to hold the vine steady, but it shook even more violently.

Keeah glanced at Eric, her eyes filled with fear. "Please be careful . . ." she began.

Eric edged farther out, then — *snap!* — the vine broke under them.

Keeah fell.

Eric leaped for her, his arms outstretched. "Grab on to me!" he cried.

On his way down, their hands met. Eric clutched Keeah's wrists, his vine pulled tight, and they swung back to the tree. Keeah grabbed the rope ladder and held it tight.

"Eric — thank you!" she gasped.

Eric's heart was still racing. "Never mind that. We need to catch whoever did this!"

Together they jumped to the ground. Julie and Neal scrambled down after them. They ran to the far tree. But they saw no one. Whoever had been shaking the vine was nowhere in sight.

Suddenly — *thumpa! thumpa!* The

ground thudded and leaves fluttered in the forest.

"It's Mr. Invisible!" said Neal. "After him!"

The kids tore through the bushes. The leaves crashed this way and that. They nearly caught up to the invisible creature, but lost the trail when it hooked out of the forest into the arena.

"There must be a thousand people here," said Julie as they pushed into the bustling crowd.

"Keep looking for clues," said Eric.

"I'm looking," whispered Neal. "But so far, I haven't spotted anything —"

"Wait!" said Keeah. "Look there, footprints!"

As they watched, large footprints appeared one after another on the ground nearby. The prints wove carefully through the crowd and led to a wagon.

A yellow wagon.

Tarok's wagon.

"Aha!" Julie said with a gasp. "I knew Tarok was a part of this."

"But what is Tarok up to?" Keeah asked. "And why is he doing what he's doing?"

All of a sudden — *honka-honka!* — a noise rose up out over the crowd.

"Come one! Come all!" a familiar voice bellowed. "See Droon's funny man! I am Tarok the clown! My act is so funny, you'll just *die* laughing!"

Droon's Funniest Man?

Honka! Honka!

The crowd cheered as Tarok ran around honking his horn on a small stage near the wagon.

"Welcome, one and all!" the little man called out. Then he pointed directly at Keeah. "I see we have Queen Relna's daughter here! And what rhymes with daughter? How about . . . water!"

Tarok then picked up a bucket with the

word *water* written on the side, rushed at the audience, and emptied it over them.

Everyone screamed and ducked.

But it wasn't water, it was glitter. It showered gently over the crowd.

"Now watch this!" said Tarok as he began to juggle three glass balls while standing on one foot. "Isn't this amazing?"

"I wish I could juggle," Neal whispered.

Julie gave him a look as the kids crept forward. "Neal, we think he's the bad guy."

Neal shrugged. "But juggling is so cool."

Tarok caught the balls and stuffed them in a pocket. "And now for something mystical and mysterious!" he boomed.

He raised his hands and — *poof!*

A cloud of red smoke exploded on the stage.

When the smoke cleared, Slag was standing there. All seven feet of him. The crowd cheered.

"Mr. Invisible, live and in person!" Neal said.

Eric snorted. "Mystical and mysterious, huh? It looks like magic to me."

Keeah frowned. "So it was Slag who tried to knock me off the vine? And it was him chasing my mother?"

Tarok waved his hands at the crowd. "I am pleased to present Slag, the mightiest man in Droon. Slag, show them — especially the little ones — just how strong you are. . . ."

Slag squinted out over the crowd, then fixed his eyes on the kids. As he did, he began to bend a long iron bar. He groaned, he growled, he snarled, he grunted. When he was done, the bar was twisted into a giant knot.

Neal nudged Eric. "Do you get the feeling he wants to do that to us?"

"He's trying to scare us," said Keeah.

"Because we suspect them of . . . of . . . oh, my gosh! She's here. . . . My mother is here!"

Eric whirled on his heels. "Where? Do you see her?"

"No," Keeah whispered, closing her eyes. "She's . . . trapped. She's hurt. I feel it. . . ."

Julie slapped her forehead. "Of course!"

"Of course what?" said Neal.

"It all makes sense now," Julie whispered. "That big net Slag had. Tarok saying they were going fishing. This weird wagon of theirs. Mr. Invisible. Don't you see?"

"Yes!" said Neal. Then he shook his head. "Well, not really."

Julie pulled the kids close. "Tarok and Slag are the ones who trapped Queen Relna! Not only that, they have her in their wagon!"

Keeah's eyes grew wide. "I'm going in there."

Eric saw blue sparks shoot suddenly from the tips of Keeah's fingers. "We're all going in," he said. "Together."

"Yeah, we'll bust them good," Neal added.

They started edging away from the crowd.

"Stop!" Tarok snapped, pointing a sharp finger at the kids. "Don't go. The fun is just beginning. I need a volunteer. You there with the silly grin. I need you!"

The crowd turned to Neal.

"Who, me?" Neal pointed to himself. "No, sorry. I don't volunteer. It always gets me in trouble. Like the time I cleaned the erasers for Mrs. Michaels and got chalk dust all over her clothes? I nearly got detention. Or the time I —"

Eric pulled him close. "Neal, this is the perfect plan! Tarok will probably just pretend to pull eggs from your ear or something."

"I don't want eggs in my ear!" Neal cried.

"But you can keep an eye on Tarok and Slag, while we snoop inside their mystery wagon," Julie pleaded. "It's the only way."

"Maybe he'll teach you to juggle," whispered Eric.

"Really? Juggle?" Neal blinked. "Okay." He jumped onto the stage.

"Right this way," Tarok said as Neal stumbled up next to him. "We'll do a bit of simple illusion. Simple and fun."

"It's magic, make no mistake," Keeah whispered to her friends. "Come on."

As they began to circle around the crowd, Tarok brought out the three glass balls again.

"Cool," Neal mumbled. He seemed entranced when Tarok started to juggle them once more.

"Keep your eye on the balls," said Tarok. "And one . . . and two . . . and —"

POOF! A great puff of red smoke exploded on the stage. And the three of them were gone.

Tarok, Slag, and Neal.

Gone in a puff of smoke!

Julie gasped. "Where's Neal? Wait a second. I don't like this after all."

Eric watched the smoke rise then begin to fall over the amazed crowd. He didn't like it, either. "Keeah," he said, "is Neal okay? Keeah?"

But the princess had already crept around to the back of Tarok's wagon.

The door creaked once, and she was inside.

Seven

Tarok's Mystery Wagon

When Eric and Julie pulled open the wagon door, they found the inside room empty.

Julie frowned. "Where did Keeah go?"

There was a small door on the opposite wall.

"Did she go back out?" asked Eric. "Oh, man. First Neal, now Keeah. We keep losing people. Let's stick close."

Julie nodded. She crossed to the small

door and pulled it open slowly. As she did, the air seemed to hum and sparkle.

"Holy cow!" she exclaimed.

Eric peeked over her shoulder. He gulped.

The door didn't lead back outside.

It led . . . to another room. And what a room!

It was at least twice the size of their school classroom. And the ceiling was three times as high as the wagon itself!

"No wonder they could fit a pilka in here," Julie whispered when they stepped in. "They could fit a whole herd of them!"

But it sure didn't look like a stable.

The place was magnificently decorated, as if it were a room in the richest palace. Candles on the walls lit an area of couches, tables, and chairs sitting on a fancy carpet.

Piled along the walls were big traveling chests. They overflowed with gold and

jewels and leather bags filled with glittering coins.

Eric shook his head slowly. "Okay, this
is plain crazy. How can you have a wagon
that's bigger on the inside than the outside?"

"Keeah was right," said Julie. "This is
no simple illusion. This is magic. Look,
there's another door at the far end. Keeah?
Keeah!"

Julie ran for the door, but Eric's eye was
caught by one chest with jewels tumbling
out.

He leaned over. Among the jewels in
the chest was a shiny black gem. It was flat
and perfectly round.

He picked it up. It glimmered in the
candlelight. Then it flickered suddenly in
his hand.

"Check this out!" he said. "It looks like

a story stone from Keeah's harp. Julie?" He glanced up.

Julie was staring through the far door. "Eric," she whispered. "Get over here. Now!"

He pushed the stone into his pocket and went to her. He stared past her through the doorway.

"Okay, well, um, this is different," he said.

"Different?" said Julie. "It's weirder than weird."

They were standing at the top of a set of steps that curved down a long way into darkness. The steps seemed to go far below the ground that the wagon was sitting on.

"I guess we have to go down?" Julie asked.

"I guess we do," said Eric.

Quietly, the two friends tramped down the steps. The stairs were covered with a kind of thick slime. They kept curving downward.

"I wish Neal were here —" said Julie.

"Me, too."

"— so he could go first!" Julie finished.

Eric tried to laugh. He couldn't. He was scared.

What had happened to Neal? And where were they going? And who *were* Tarok and Slag, anyway?

Finally, the steps ended. Eric and Julie came out into a stone chamber. The floor was wet. And it smelled like the beach.

Like seawater.

It was much darker and colder than the other rooms. But Eric breathed a sigh of relief.

Keeah was there.

And she was not alone.

"Mother . . . Mother . . ." she murmured.

Keeah was standing next to a cage. The red tiger lay inside, almost still, breathing very slowly.

"I feel so helpless!" she said. "Look at her. She's sick. She can hardly breathe."

"Maybe it's because she needs to change into another shape," said Eric. "And she can't because of the cage."

"She needs to be set free," said Julie.

Keeah reached her hand toward the cage.

Kkkkk! A bolt of red light shot out from the bars and struck Keeah's hand. She snatched it back. "This is a sorcerer's magic! Red light is always a sign of dark magic."

"You should know. . . ." said a cold voice.

Tarok strode from the shadows. Gone

was his clown's nose. His wild blue hair. His silly horn.

He tossed up a glass ball and caught it. "So you've found our little secret. Quite a catch, isn't she? The Queen of Droon. In my little wagon."

"Let her go!" demanded Keeah.

"Mmm . . . no," Tarok replied.

"You know," snarled Eric, "for a funny man, you're not very funny."

Tarok's face twisted into a dark scowl. "No, the fun is over. Now the games begin. Want to play catch?"

Tarok held the ball up in front of Eric.

That's when the kids noticed a tiny shape inside the ball. A shape they all knew.

It was waving at them.

"Oh, my gosh," said Eric. "It's Neal!"

Julie gasped. "You let him out of there! Right now!"

"No," said Tarok, backing away. "Slag, come forward!"

The giant stepped out of the shadows behind Tarok. He held his pretzel-shaped iron bar.

"I bend you like a bar," Slag grunted.

Eric glanced at Keeah and Julie. "I was right. This is definitely *not* funny!"

The Quest Begins!

Tarok stepped over to the cage and waved his hand over it.

Kkkkk! In a violent burst of light, the cage was empty, and Tarok was holding a second ball.

In the ball was the red tiger.

"How did you do that?" demanded Keeah. "Where did you get that power?"

"Yeah!" Eric growled. "Just who *are* you?"

Tarok stepped back toward the shadows. "We're just two fellows with a job to finish. . . ."

"That's right," said Slag. "She'd be mad at us if we failed."

"She?" said Julie. "She who?"

Keeah's eyes widened. She began to tremble.

"Witch Demither!" she hissed. "She's where they get their power!"

"How very clever of you, Princess," Tarok said, bowing slightly. "We do odd jobs for the witch, it's true. We're her *legs*, I guess you could say. Demither told us to catch the tiger, so . . ."

"I caught her," grunted Slag. "Me and my net. In the woods."

"Of course!" said Eric. "You came straight out of the water. That's where Demither rules. And this magic wagon . . . it even smells like fish!"

"Ha!" Tarok laughed. "Using Demither's magic, we'll have more than fish. We'll win the Quest and the prize, a fabulous treasure of gold and jewels! It's our reward for catching the queen."

"You're evil!" Julie cried. "You're not allowed to use magic here. Especially witch magic!"

Then — *bong!* — Ortha's gong sounded outside, signaling that the Quest was about to begin.

"I'd love to stay and chat," Tarok said, "but Demither wants the queen and we want that prize! Oh, I almost forgot . . . catch —"

Taking the ball with Neal inside, he tossed it up to the high ceiling.

"Don't break Neal!" cried Julie. She jumped for the ball. But somewhere near the ceiling it burst. Neal popped out — full size — and collapsed to the floor.

Tarok and Slag leaped away into the shadows.

"They're escaping!" said Keeah. "After them!"

Suddenly, the walls around the kids began to collapse. *Flonk! Clang!* The room got smaller.

"Let's get out before it traps us!" cried Eric.

He helped Neal up and they all jumped after Tarok but — *splat!* — they found themselves facedown in the mud outside the wagon.

Flap! Blonk! Plink! The wagon kept changing.

"It's becoming . . . a chariot!" cried Julie.

The great gong sounded once more.

"The Quest is starting!" yelled Neal.

Tarok laughed icily. He snapped the reins hard and his pilka charged into the arena.

Keeah's fingers sparked. "I'll stop them!"

"No, Keeah, don't do it," said Eric, rushing to her. "We'll stop them the regular way."

"Yeah," said Neal, running over to her chariot. "We'll chase them!"

Keeah stared at the chariot, then at her friends. Then she gave them a smile. "Let's go!"

The kids hopped into the chariot. Galen's pilka, Leep, was already hitched up to it. Keeah snapped the reins and the chariot thundered onto the race course.

Whoosh! A cloud of dust blossomed up from the starting line as a dozen other chariots raced around the arena.

But Tarok and Slag were far in the lead. Their chariot charged ahead, rounded the arena, and shot into the forest.

Already the sun was falling behind the trees.

"We have to catch him soon," Julie said, "or we'll be too late. The island will be gone."

"Faster, Leep!" Keeah said, and the pilka jumped ahead with a burst of speed.

Eric gripped the sides of the chariot tighter. "It's okay to go fast, but please drive safely!"

Leaves and vines flapped and whizzed by as they drove deeper into the forest. Right, left, right. The course twisted and turned sharply.

The path grew narrow. Then something loomed ahead of them.

It was the first of the obstacles.

"Uh-oh. Flame walls ahead!" Neal called out. "Prepare to be charcoal broiled!"

A wall of orange flame rose up on each

side of the narrowing path. The fire lashed out like fingers trying to claw whatever passed through.

But Tarok didn't slow down.

He shot a handful of silver dust into the path, and — *k-k-k-zing!* — the flames froze instantly.

"Thank you for your magic, Demither!" he said as he drove his chariot swiftly between the frozen flames.

As soon as he passed through, the fire crackled angrily to life again.

Hrrr! Leep reared up, nearly tipping the chariot over. She wouldn't go on. She stamped her feet on the ground and began backing up.

"She won't ride into the flames!" Keeah said.

Julie looked around. "I have an idea. I saw it in a movie once. Wish me luck —"

"Luck!" said Eric.

Julie pulled two leaves from a nearby bush, jumped up onto Leep's back, and slapped the leaves over the pilka's head so it couldn't see sideways.

"Try it now!" Julie called back.

Keeah urged Leep to move forward.

Hrrr! Leep whinnied loudly, then raced between the fiery walls and out the other side.

"Yes!" Julie whipped the leaves off.

Eric helped her back into the chariot and slapped her a high five. "Nice work, Julie!"

"The next one's up to you guys," she said.

Keeah drove the chariot hard over the path.

Eric looked ahead even as he clutched the sides of the chariot more tightly.

He knew — they all knew — that they needed to do more than stop Tarok and Slag. They had to win the prize. Eric remembered Galen's words. For the one meant to win, the prize was what he or she wanted most.

Eric knew what Keeah wanted. It's what they all wanted. A cure for Queen Relna.

But it sure wasn't going to be easy!

Clank! Plonk! Slag began tossing iron bars out the back of their speeding chariot. The bars struck the path and bounced up at the kids.

Keeah tried to drive the chariot around the bars, but one of them hit a wheel. The chariot bounced. So did Eric and Neal. They shot out of the chariot like cannonballs from a cannon.

"Whoooa!" cried Eric as they went

hurtling toward a tree. "We're gonna get smushed!"

Suddenly — *fwing!* — a thick net of vines flashed down from above. Eric tumbled into the net unhurt. Neal shot in next to him. They looked up. A handful of green Bangledorn monkeys waved from the high trees. "Yee-yee!"

"Thanks!" Eric yelled up.

"It's nice to have friends in high places!" Neal added.

Eric and Neal leaped down from the net just as their chariot passed underneath. *Plop! Plop!* They dropped down right next to Julie and Keeah.

"Glad to have you back!" said Keeah, laughing.

Then another laugh broke through the forest.

"This will stop you!" Tarok yelled back as he sped into the next turn in the course.

"What will stop us?" asked Julie.

Then they heard it.

Sploosh! Crash! Splash!

"Oh, no!" cried Keeah. "The raging river!"

Nine

Island of Magic

A wild river crashed and surged across the course, sending cold white spray high in the air.

Tarok slowed his wagon only long enough to shoot more sparkly dust across the water.

K-k-k-zing! The river turned as smooth as glass. It froze into a flat road of ice.

"Aha!" Slag cheered, snapping hard on

the reins and driving their pilka across the ice.

"Hurry," said Julie. "Maybe we can get across before he changes it back —"

Too late. *Splursh!* The river exploded again into whitecapped rapids the instant Tarok and Slag reached the far side.

Keeah pulled Leep to a stop on the near bank and jumped out of the chariot. "We can't fail at this. We need to get the prize. We need to!"

"We won't fail," said Julie. "We'll just have to get across the old-fashioned way."

Neal stepped back from the churning river bank. "You want us to swim across *that?*"

Julie smiled. "Not if we can help it!" She pointed up. Above their heads were dozens of long, thick vines hanging down from the tall trees.

"We swing across to the far side," she said.

"Oh, man," sighed Neal. "It's like I never left gym class." Then he shrugged. "But, hey, you gotta do what you gotta do."

They each grabbed a long vine, ran back, and leaped from the ground.

Fwit! Fwit! Fwit! Fwit! The four friends soared over the river's crashing waves.

Plop! Plop! Plop! Plop! They landed safely on the far bank. They picked themselves up and plowed through one last row of trees.

Beyond them lay a strip of white sandy beach.

On the beach, jutting out into the water, was a narrow footbridge.

And Tarok's chariot was racing toward it.

"We'll have to go the rest of the way on foot," said Keeah. "Come on. Let's run like the wind."

The four friends raced across the sand as fast as they could. At first, the black sea seemed peaceful and almost golden in the fading light.

But as they drew nearer, the water rumbled and the ground quaked. The sea churned wildly, spitting up large, white-capped waves.

"The island," Keeah said. "It's coming!"

Ka-fooom! The sea broke open and a rocky point of land came thrusting up from the black depths. It was as if a small mountain were being pushed out of the earth, through the water, and into the light of day.

Waves bubbled and hissed and swirled all around the land, then went calm.

In the center of the island was a perfectly white stone. On the stone lay a wooden bowl.

It was plain and battered.

It was not encrusted with jewels or gold.

It had no markings on it.

It was just a bowl.

But the instant the fading sunlight struck it, the air around it turned a hundred colors.

The bowl itself glowed and sparkled.

And so did the water in the bowl.

"Oh, my gosh," said Keeah, racing to the bridge. "That's the prize. . . ."

Eric could tell — they could all tell — it wasn't just seawater rippling in a simple wooden bowl.

It was what the true winner wanted most.

"Keeah, the prize is for you," said Eric.

"If Tarok were meant to win, it would be a pile of treasure. But it's not. It must be . . . the cure."

"Run," said the princess. "Run! RUN!"

They raced across the footbridge as fast as their legs could carry them.

But it wasn't fast enough.

Tarok and Slag reached the end of the bridge and leaped onto the island.

"The prize!" Tarok howled, raising his arms in victory. "The prize is mine!"

Ten

A Spell from the Past

Tarok grabbed the bowl from the stone. He stared at it.

"What's this?" he snarled. "This is the legendary prize? It's nothing but an old wooden bowl!"

"Where is the treasure?" Slag boomed. He stuck his nose in the bowl and took a sniff. "This smells like nothing! I want a real prize!"

Before the kids could get to the island,

Tarok and Slag began fighting over the bowl.

"Give it to me!" said Tarok.

"No, it's mine!" Slag boomed.

Suddenly, the bowl slipped through their fingers. It hung in the air for a moment.

Then it crashed to the ground.

Sploosh! The golden liquid splashed out, drained through the rocks, and was washed into the black sea.

"No!" Keeah gasped, jumping onto the island. "That was the prize. It was magic!"

"Magic?" said Tarok. He looked at Keeah, then at the bowl, then at Slag. "You numbskull!"

"Me?" grunted Slag. "You did it!"

The two men began to slap each other.

Keeah's fingertips shot off blue sparks. "Give me the glass ball now! My mother must change her shape or she'll die!"

Neal and Julie grabbed Tarok by the arms.

"Okay, okay!" the little man said. He tugged the glass ball from a pocket, tossed it up, and — *k-k-k-zing!* — the ball sizzled and sparked, then burst away to nothing in a puff of red smoke.

The tiger appeared before them, lying on the ground, its head resting on its giant paws.

Keeah knelt next to her.

The queen gave out a long, quivering breath. "Keeah, without the cure, only Demither has the power to alter this spell. No one else may do it."

But the princess's eyes flashed with determination. "No. There must be another way. It can't end like this!"

At that moment, Eric's pocket felt hot as if something in it were burning.

"Whoa," he said. "I totally forgot."

He dug his hand in his pocket and pulled out the black gemstone. "I found this in Tarok's wagon," he said. "It's just the right shape to be a story stone from your harp. I thought it might be one of the missing ones."

Keeah held the gem in her hand. "It *is* one of the stones," she said. "I know it is —"

The moment she touched it, the black gem began to flicker in Keeah's hand. And as it did, a halo of bright red light began to swirl around her.

Then the light covered her mother.

The tiger howled a sudden, unearthly sound.

Slag stepped back. "Red light! She has . . . witch power!"

Tarok gaped at Keeah. "But I thought only Demither could do that. The princess . . . she has Demither's power!"

Julie frowned. "For your information, Keeah is a very good wizard —"

Eric turned to Tarok and stared at him fiercely. "Where did you find this stone? Tell me!"

Tarok shriveled under Eric's gaze. "Years ago in the Panjibarrh Hills! I saw Demither and the princess alone together —"

"That's impossible!" Julie snapped. "She would never be alone with that horrible witch!"

"I saw them together," Tarok went on. "Demither held the princess's hands. Strange light flowed between them. Red light. Just like right now! That's where I found the black gem. Now — let — me — go!"

With a burst of strength, Tarok wriggled free of Julie and Neal and — *poof!* — the air filled with smoke. In the confusion, Tarok leaped to the bridge, and Slag with him. Together, they raced to the shore.

But the kids couldn't tear their eyes away from the queen. She had already begun to change.

The tail was first. Then the legs. And the back.

They all turned silvery and black.

"Keeah," the queen purred, "you have saved me. I don't know how you have the power . . . but you do have it." The queen struggled to her feet and crawled to the shore.

"Mother, is it true what Tarok said?" Keeah asked. "About the witch . . . and me?"

Relna shuddered as the last of her red fur vanished and the shiny, dark skin spread completely over her.

"That is a secret I will find the answer to," she said. "Now I must go. My next life is the darkest yet. But there will be joy on the other side. Until then, be careful . . . be well . . . I love you!"

With those words, the queen slid beneath the churning waves. The water crashed once, then was still for a long time.

"Oh, Mother . . ." Keeah whispered.

Suddenly — *splash!* — the waves broke open and something soared out.

"Queen Relna!" Julie shouted.

But this time, nothing of the tiger was left. Instead, she was a sleek and slender sea creature.

A dolphin!

As black as ink, the dolphin flew joyously over the waves. She twirled in midair, then slid beneath the sea again. Over and over she soared and dived.

Softly, Keeah said, "She's beautiful!"

"She has always been beautiful," answered a friendly voice above them.

The kids looked up to see Galen standing calmly on the edge of the bridge.

"Come now," he said. "The Quest is over. The staircase has appeared. And already the magical island begins to sink."

The kids climbed onto the bridge.

Splursh! Black waves washed over the new island, and it descended, rumbling and shaking, beneath the sea once more.

In a moment, it was gone.

On shore, Tarok and Slag climbed into their chariot. *Flonk! Blink!* — in seconds, it was a boat again. It motored quickly into the water.

"The bad guys are getting away!" cried Neal.

Galen smiled. "I think Demither has plans for them. They failed today. She won't like that!"

As soon as the boat hit the water,

waves began to toss it about, driving it far out to sea.

"Serves them right," said Julie.

The kids and Galen crossed the bridge back onto the beach, where the magical staircase stood shimmering on the rocky shore.

From the edge of the forest came a familiar shout. "Yee! Yee!"

Ortha stood with a small band of green monkeys, waving to Eric, Julie, and Neal as they raced to the stairs. The kids waved back.

At the bottom of the staircase, Galen handed the princess her harp. "Although it may not seem so, Keeah, today you have won the Quest."

She smiled and hugged Eric, Julie, and Neal. "I couldn't have done it without my friends."

Galen nodded slowly. "Truly, friends like these are also a prize."

Then Keeah set the black story stone in its place on the harp. As she did, the stone flashed for an instant. Then deep within it, as if etched into the gem from inside, was a shape.

A leaping dolphin.

"Only one stone remains to be found," said the wizard. "Only one more change, then the queen of Droon shall take her throne again."

He motioned to the stairs. "Now, quickly, children, up you go. The Upper World calls you!"

Neal laughed as he jumped onto the staircase. "What a cool Quest," he said. "I can't wait to climb ropes in gym tomorrow. Thanks to Droon, I'm pretty sure I can do anything!"

The three kids headed up the stairs for home.

"Until next time," Keeah called to them, her eyes beaming brightly. Then she and Galen turned to watch the dolphin dive and leap across the waves, all the way to the distant horizon.

"I like happy endings," said Julie, racing up to Eric's basement.

Eric flicked on the closet light.

Whoosh! The stairs disappeared beneath them.

"And happy beginnings," Neal added.

Eric grinned. "The in-between stuff is pretty cool, too. Especially when it happens in Droon!"

The Hawk Bandits
of Tarkoom

For my brother Rick,
who knows that the adventure
doesn't have to end

One

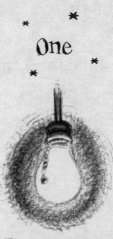

One Head Is Better Than Two

Eric Hinkle and his friend Julie carefully pulled open a small door under the stairs in his basement.

Errr-errrk! The door's old hinges squeaked.

Behind the door was a small, dark closet, with a single unlit lightbulb hanging from the ceiling.

"Isn't it weird how it looks just like a regular closet?" asked Julie.

Eric grinned. "It *is* a regular closet. To everyone else."

But to Eric, Julie, and their friend Neal, it was more than just a closet. It was the entrance to another world.

The magical world of Droon.

Actually, it was Julie who had first discovered the entrance to Droon.

She'd just gone into the closet, when suddenly the door closed behind her, the light went out, and — *whoosh!* — a long, shimmering staircase appeared where the floor had been.

The kids were scared, of course.

But the staircase looked so beautiful they just had to see what was at the bottom.

On their first visit to Droon, they met a young princess named Keeah who was now one of their best friends.

They'd also met a good wizard named

Galen Longbeard and his spider troll helper, Max.

Galen was teaching Keeah to be a wizard, too.

Together with Keeah and Galen, the kids had battled a wicked sorcerer named Lord Sparr, a strange witch called Demither, and lots of other nasty creatures who were always trying to take over Droon.

The best part was that Eric and his friends seemed to be helping Keeah keep Droon free.

"I asked you over," Eric said to Julie, "because I think we need to keep the closet in good working condition. After all, it's our only way into Droon."

"Great idea," said Julie. "If the door squeaks too much, your parents will hear us. And Galen told us always to keep Droon a secret."

"I'll put in a fresh lightbulb," said Eric.

"You can oil the hinges. I asked Neal to come and sweep up, but he's late."

"As usual!" Julie said with a laugh.

She took an oilcan from the workbench. Standing on her toes, she began oiling the door's hinges. Eric searched the nearby cabinets for a new lightbulb to replace the old one.

As they worked, Eric recalled their latest visits to Droon. He and his friends had had many adventures. But they'd also uncovered many mysteries.

For one thing, Keeah said she remembered being in the Upper World — Eric's world — a long time ago.

But that didn't seem possible.

Then, Keeah was told that Witch Demither secretly gave her some powers. Witch powers!

Keeah didn't remember that at all.

"Hey, Eric," said Julie, bending down to

oil the lower hinges, "what do you think witch powers are like?"

"I was just thinking about that!" said Eric.

"I mean, are they dark and dangerous like Lord Sparr's?" she asked. "Or more like the sort of natural wizard things Galen can do?"

"I don't know." Eric found a new light-bulb and took it to the closet. "But wouldn't it be weird if there was a connection between Keeah being here and having witch powers? I wonder if Galen knows."

"Galen's five hundred and forty-two years old!" said Julie. "If he doesn't know, who does?"

Eric shrugged. "Maybe we will. If we ever get to Droon again."

He glanced at a soccer ball sitting on the workbench. After their first visit to Droon, Keeah had put a spell on it. When the ball

★ 213 ★

floated in the air, it meant the staircase would be open for them.

"I can't wait to go —" Eric began.

Just then, four furry white paws trotted past the window. They were followed by two beat-up sneakers.

"Get back here!" cried a familiar voice.

"*Woof!*" came the response.

"It's Neal," said Eric.

"And Snorky," added Julie. Then she laughed. "Looks like Neal's having trouble with him . . . again."

"We'd better help him out!" said Eric. The two kids dropped everything and rushed up the basement stairs, through the kitchen, and out to the backyard.

When they got there, Neal was on all fours, nose to nose with Snorky, trying to grab him.

Julie giggled. "It looks like you're dancing!"

"It's not funny," Neal groaned as Snorky romped away to sniff a tree. "I was teaching him to fetch when he escaped!"

Eric tried to trap Snorky from behind. "What was he fetching?"

"A box of cookies," Neal said.

Julie shook her head. "Only *you* would think of teaching a dog to fetch food for you."

Neal grinned. "What can I say? I'm a genius."

"Hey, genius, your dog just ran into my house!" said Eric. He jumped up the steps and into the kitchen.

Inside, Snorky skittered under the table and headed down the hall at top speed, tracking dirty paw prints the whole way.

"Not the living room!" said Eric. "My mom just vacuumed!"

"We'll trap him in the hall," Neal shouted, dashing through the kitchen.

Eric and Julie tore around the other way. But Eric slipped on the carpet, slid across the floor, and crashed down — *ka-thunk!* — taking Julie and a large house-plant with him.

The plant spilled dirt all over the carpet.

"Woof! Woof!" barked Snorky as he turned and shot down the stairs to the basement.

"Oh, no!" said Eric, scrambling to his feet. "What if Snorky gets into the closet?"

"Let's get down there right away!" said Julie.

But when they entered the basement, they stopped short.

Julie gasped softly. "Oh, my gosh!"

The soccer ball was floating in the air over the workbench.

"Keeah needs us in Droon," said Eric. "That means the stairs will be open for us."

"And for Snorky —" said Neal. "Uh-oh!"

The three friends spun around to see Snorky's curly tail disappear behind the closet door.

Click. The door closed softly.

"Yikes!" cried Neal. "He's going to Droon!"

"But he can't unless the light is out," said Eric.

He pulled open the door. The light *was* out.

"Oh, man! I didn't put the new bulb in!"

Below them, the stairs were shimmering in a rainbow of colors. And Snorky was prancing down them, his tail wagging happily.

"Come back here, you," said Julie.

The three friends dashed down the stairs, but Snorky began to run. *"Woof! Woof!"* he barked.

"He thinks it's a game!" moaned Neal.

As they descended through the clouds, the sky over Droon was turning from black to purple.

"It's just before morning," said Julie. "It should be getting light soon."

They jumped off the bottom of the staircase and looked around. Dusty brown mountains surrounded them on every side.

"It looks like the Panjibarrh hills," said Eric. "We've been here before. . . ."

"Never mind that," said Neal, scanning the rocky ground. "Where's Snorky? Snorky! Get back here. You need to go home —"

Then the staircase faded. The kids knew it would not reappear until it was time to go home.

"Too late to send Snorky back," said Julie.

Grrrr. Something was growling from behind a rock.

"Snorky?" said Eric cautiously. "Is that you?"

Grrrr! The growling was louder this time.

"Here, puppy," said Neal softly. "Here —"

A head peered from behind the rock.

But it wasn't Snorky's head.

It was large and gray. Its features were craggy and its skin was rough, as if it were very old.

Grrrr! Another head, the same as the first, jerked up from behind the rock.

"There are two of them!" said Eric, backing up. "Oh, man, we are cooked!"

The first head moved out from behind the rock and the second one moved with it. That's when they saw that both heads were on the same neck!

"That's definitely *not* Snorky," said Neal.

The beast growled, opening both sets of jaws. Four rows of huge fangs dripped a thick, yellow liquid.

Julie stepped back. "That is so — ewww!"

"Don't make it mad," Eric whispered.

GRR-RRR! The twin heads roared again.

"Too late for that," mumbled Neal.

The creature stomped toward them, then stood for a moment, roaring and growling.

Then it leaped at them.

What the Legend Says

"Get down!" Eric cried, grabbing Julie and Neal. The three friends dove behind a large boulder just as the beast pounced.

Thoom! It shook the ground when it landed. Then it turned quickly.

"It's coming at us again!" said Julie.

Suddenly — *hrrrr!* — a six-legged, shaggy animal called a pilka thundered into the clearing.

"Stay back, you hideous thing!" cried a voice.

The kids looked up. Princess Keeah sat atop the pilka, her gold crown blazing in the dim light. She charged over the rocks at the beast.

"Keeah, watch out!" Eric shouted.

But Keeah rode forward, staring down the beast, her eyes blazing. "Begone!" she cried. "Or I'll . . . I'll . . . oh!"

Her left hand suddenly glowed with a sizzling red light. An instant later, a blast of red sparks knocked the two-headed creature back.

Eeeoow! Both heads howled angrily at her. Then, shrinking back, the beast clambered away through the rocks. In a moment, it was gone.

Just then, the great orange sun flickered over the mountaintops, and the purple sky brightened to pink. Morning had come to Droon.

"Wow, Keeah, that was awesome!" said Neal, jumping out from behind the boulder. "It was like that thing actually *obeyed* you!"

The princess slid down from the saddle and hugged her friends tightly. "I'm not sure why it did. But I'm glad it did! Are you all right?"

Eric breathed out in relief. "I think so. But in another second we would have been two-headed-dog food!"

"*Woof?*"

"Snorky!" Neal cried, whirling on his heels.

Trembling, the small dog stumbled toward the friends and leaped into Julie's arms.

"Poor Snorky," she said. "He's shaking."

"He's *my* pet, you know!" Neal grumbled. "I'm starting to think he doesn't really like me."

Keeah smiled. "Come on, everyone. I called you here because yesterday an earthquake rocked the Panjibarrh hills. King Batamogi found something strange and wants us to see. Galen's caravan is just ahead. Let's go meet him. We need to tell him about this beast!"

As the sun climbed over Panjibarrh's famous dust hills, the four friends rode Keeah's pilka down to the valley below.

Before long, they spotted two figures traveling across the plains.

"There's Galen!" said Julie. "And Max, too!"

Galen, his long white beard flowing above a blue cloak stitched all over with stars and moons, rode the head pilka. A tall cone-shaped wizard hat sat on his head.

Behind him rode Max, his spider troll helper. Max had eight furry legs, a pug nose, and wild orange hair. Two other pilkas were laden with supplies and saddlebags bulging with books.

"Hail, friends from the Upper World!" said Galen as the children rode up. "What news?"

"A two-headed beast attacked us!" said Eric.

Galen frowned. "Two-headed, you say?"

"And both heads were pretty ugly," said Neal.

The wizard stroked his beard as the children took turns describing the beast.

"It seemed old, yet it moved very quickly," said Keeah. "Luckily, I stopped it."

"Its four eyes were red and scary," Julie said.

"Also, it had fangs the size of bananas," said Eric. "Have you ever heard of such a thing?"

The wizard looked out over the hills. "I have," he said. "But what you say fills me with fear."

"Why?" asked Julie.

"Because," said Galen, "the beast you describe died four hundred years ago! Now, follow me. Quickly!"

With that, Galen snapped the reins of his pilka and tore ahead. The children stared at one another for a moment, then followed Galen into the hills. They didn't stop until they came to the place where a quake had split the ground wide open.

"So!" said Galen, staring at the jagged crack. "As I feared, this was no normal earthquake."

"Over here, my friends!" called a voice.

A furry creature with a whiskery snout and long, foxlike ears waved from atop a rock. He wore a green crown and a short green cape.

It was Batamogi, one of the ten kings who ruled the Oobja people of Panjibarrh. He jumped down from the rock and bowed first to Galen and Princess Keeah, then to Eric and his friends.

"A big rumbly-rumble shook the hills yesterday," Batamogi told them. "It sent me flying out of bed. I've been shaking ever since! This morning I found it. I called you here right away."

"Found *it*?" said Eric. "What did you find?"

Batamogi pointed to the deep gash in the earth. "An ancient tomb. See for yourselves!"

Galen dismounted his pilka and strode

over to the split in the ground. The wizard was very old, but he moved nimbly over the rocks and down into the ruined tomb.

At the bottom was a small square of earth. Pressed into the earth was the outline of a beast.

A beast that was not there.

A beast with two heads.

"Holy cow!" Julie gasped. "This must be the grave of the great-great-grandfather of that monster we saw."

"No, it *was* the monster you saw," said Galen, his eyes fixed on the outline. "This earthquake was no accident. It was ancient magic that opened the beast's tomb and set it free."

Keeah turned to Galen. "I thought it died a long time ago. Do you mean it didn't really die?"

The wizard did not answer. Instead, he

inspected every inch of the tomb. Finally, he climbed out and dusted his hands.

"The beast is called Kem," Galen said. "It was created by a magic as old as Droon itself. Long ago I fought the beast and buried it here, thinking it was dead. I was wrong, fooled by the dark magic. In his prime, Kem was watchdog of the old city of Tarkoom. He howled like a ghost before attacking intruders."

Eric and Neal shivered at the same time.

"Tarkoom?" squeaked Max. "That was a place of thieves! And robbers!"

"And terrible bandits!" said Batamogi, scratching his ears nervously. "But Tarkoom was destroyed ages ago. You can still see the ruins."

Galen pulled a thick scroll from his saddlebag. "True," he said solemnly. "I was there the night it fell. A great fire reduced the city to rubble."

"Good!" said Julie. "Serves it right."

Galen unrolled the scroll and read it. "Ah, but here lies the problem. A legend says that centuries may pass, but if ever Kem should howl again, Tarkoom would rise from its ashes."

"The city would just come back?" asked Neal.

Galen nodded. "And all the terrible creatures who lived there. Droon's old magic is powerful."

Keeah took a breath, looked at her friends, then back at Galen. "So, what do we do now?"

"We wait in the hills above the Pan-jibarrh Valley," said the wizard, rolling up his scroll again. "If Tarkoom does rise again, we'll have a most important job ahead of us. Until then, we wait and watch."

Eric frowned. "What exactly will we see?"

"The past," said Galen. "We will see the dark past of Droon coming back!"

Three

Tarkoom . . . Again!

For the next hour, Batamogi led the small troop up one dusty path and down another. They were heading for the highest point in all the Panjibarrh hills.

"Who lived in Tarkoom?" Julie asked.

"Hawk bandits, they were called," Galen said, fixing his eyes on the road ahead. "Half human, half bird. As terrifying to see as they were ruthless. But worst of all was their leader, Ving."

Batamogi nodded, shivering. "The stories say he possessed a strange, soothing voice. It made his victims feel safe. Then he swooped down on heavy wings — *fwit! fwit!* — and robbed them of everything! Oh, Ving and his bandits were feared across all of Droon."

"Until my master stopped them!" said Max, beaming proudly.

"Four hundred years ago," said Galen, his pale cheeks blushing. "But now we must do it again. You see, Tarkoom was a city in the ancient empire of Goll, an evil realm of dark magic from Droon's earliest times. After a long struggle, Goll — like Tarkoom itself — was destroyed."

"But its magic still lives!" Max added.

Galen nodded. "Indeed it does. If Ving and his bandits come to life and work their evil on present-day Droon, I fear the whole dark past of Goll may live again. If I am right, we must stop Ving from changing our world in any way —"

The earth trembled suddenly.

"Another rumbly-rumble!" said Batamogi as Snorky jumped into his arms.

Galen stopped his pilka on a ridge and looked down. "And here we are!"

Below them lay the vast Panjibarrh Valley.

In it were piles of rock, crumbled stones, broken columns, sunken streets, and collapsed buildings.

"Tarkoom," said Batamogi under his breath.

"That's the place?" said Neal, looking down at the ruined city. "Doesn't look too lively."

The earth trembled beneath their feet again.

"Just wait . . ." the wizard said. "Even

now, Tarkoom prepares to return. Let us make camp."

The eight adventurers made a small encampment in a clearing overlooking the ruined city.

Galen sat on a boulder with his scroll and took up the watch.

Max watered the pilkas, while Keeah unpacked some snacks and passed them out.

"Food, anyone?" she asked.

"*Woof!*" barked Snorky.

"It figures!" said Neal, shaking his head. "'Food' is the only word he understands."

"Oh, is that so?" said Batamogi, turning to Snorky and scruffing him. "Well, let's just see!"

The Oobja king let Snorky sniff the cuff of his sleeve. "Now, Snorky, stay here. . . ."

Batamogi backed up slowly, then scurried off behind some big boulders. A moment later, he called out, "Snorky . . . fetch!"

In a flash, Snorky bounded up and, sniffing along the ground, trotted away into the rocks.

A moment later Batamogi waddled back to the camp with Snorky nipping at his heels. "Ho-ho!"

"That was awesome!" said Neal. "Snorky, now me!" He went and hid himself among the rocks. "Snorky . . . fetch!"

The dog went over to Max, curled up, yawned, and fell asleep. Then he began to snore.

"Poor Neal!" said Keeah when Neal returned glumly. "I'm sure Snorky likes you very much, in his own way."

Hours went by. The day wore on into evening. And still Galen read the scroll, kept watch, and said nothing.

"It's getting cool," said Keeah. "I wish we had . . ." All of a sudden — *fwoosh!* — a small fire appeared before them, its flames crackling. The princess jumped back.

"Where did that come from?" she said.

For the first time in hours, Galen moved, looking over at the princess. "You did that, Keeah," he said. "It is one of your *other* powers."

Eric shot a look at Julie. They both remembered what they had spoken about earlier that day. That Keeah had . . . *witch* powers.

"We may never know how you got these powers," said Galen, "but you must learn to control them."

Keeah frowned. "I'm sorry. They seem to come from nowhere and just . . . happen."

"Like when you helped your mother

change from a tiger to a dolphin?" asked Julie, remembering their last adventure in Droon.

"Or when you scared Kem away," said Neal.

Keeah nodded. "It frightens me a little. Well, a lot. The magic seems very strong. And wild. I'm afraid I might hurt someone."

"Pah! Never!" said Max firmly. "You are a very fine young wizard. And I don't believe you were ever alone with any witches. Besides, your father says it's impossible —"

"That mystery must wait, Keeah," Galen said, standing quickly. "Tarkoom . . . begins to wake!"

As the last streaks of sunlight cut across the ruined stones, the valley rumbled even more.

Once. Twice. A third time.

The piles of old rubble and broken stones shivered and shook and rocked and rattled.

Finally — *ka-phooom!* — the ground quaked from one end of the valley to the other.

And it happened.

The toppled stones of the wrecked city of Tarkoom seemed to fly up one by one and set themselves neatly back into place.

Columns, walls, towers, gardens!

Stone by stone, Tarkoom was rebuilding itself from its own ruins!

"Oh, my gosh," Julie exclaimed. "It's coming back. Tarkoom is coming back!"

Four

City of Bandits

As they all watched, the centuries-old city of Tarkoom shuddered slowly into the present.

Where rocks had lain scattered on the plain, now great buildings stood.

Dusty piles of tumbled stones were now the sturdy towers and turrets of a monumental city.

Tarkoom was back, glowing within high walls of red- and honey-colored stone.

And at its center stood a giant domed palace.

"It's beautiful," said Keeah under her breath.

"Beautiful, perhaps," said Galen. "But full of bandits who will try to stop us from doing what we must do."

"So," said Neal, "*their* mission will be to stop *our* mission. But what exactly *is* our mission?"

The wizard let a smile crease his lips as he tapped his scroll. "My friends, we must do nothing less than destroy Tarkoom!"

"The whole city?" asked Eric. "But how?"

"We must somehow use Ving's own plan against him," the wizard replied. "The legend is most specific about this. If I am right, he will mount an attack tonight. If he succeeds, he will have altered Droon in our time. He and his bandits will have become part of it."

"Oh, dear!" said Batamogi. "An attack! I hope not on my poor people!"

"But we'll stop him," said Keeah firmly.

"Only if we hurry!" said Galen.

Leaving their pilkas at the camp, the band of eight travelers climbed down into the valley.

For most of the way, the only sound was their own careful plodding through mountain passes. And the sound of Snorky whimpering.

At last, the narrow way opened up to an awesome sight. Galen held up his hand.

"The entrance to Tarkoom!" he declared.

Hewn from the face of a cliff was a large arched opening. It soared up from the ground as high as two houses. Its sides were cut into the red stone and glowed crimson in the moonlight.

"Awesome," said Eric. "But scary. Look."

Above the opening, a giant hawk head was carved into the cliff wall.

Its eyes were shimmering jewels that seemed to stare down on anyone who might enter.

"That is the image of Ving, leader of the bandits," said Galen. "He loves only himself."

"No kidding," Neal mumbled. "It's like having a picture of yourself on your front door!"

"Let us enter," said Galen softly.

The moment he set foot through the arch — *eeoow!* — the howling of the two-headed beast rose up from deep within the city streets.

"Kem is doing his job," Keeah said with a shiver. "He really is the city's watchdog."

"Which means the bandits will soon know we're here," said Julie. "Be careful, everyone."

They passed into a street lined by columns of polished red stone. The buildings on either side were carved deep into the valley cliffs.

The black holes of their doors and windows were like eerie eyes staring out of the past.

"Everything looks so new," said Keeah. "It almost feels as if we're going back in time."

Galen shook his head. "No, Tarkoom has invaded the present. At this very moment, Ving sits in his palace, hatching his terrible plot to stay in our world."

"And staying in our world," said Batamogi, "means the dark past of Droon will come again!"

"That's why we need to destroy the city!" Max chirped. "So the past will leave the present and go back to the past so our present will be safe for the future!"

Neal blinked. "Will there be a quiz on this? Because I'm getting a major headache."

Eric tried to laugh, but he couldn't. He didn't quite understand it, either.

He paused to sort it out in his head.

"Okay," he mumbled, counting on his fingers. "One, Tarkoom is a city from the past, right? But, two, the earthquake sort of released it from the past, and now, three, it's in the present. Okay, it's some magic thing that only happens in Droon. Now we need to — four — find out what Ving is up to and — five — stop him. Then, six, we wreck the city so it goes back to the past where it belongs. Neal, is that right? Does that make sense to you? Neal?"

Eric looked up from his hands. He was alone.

The others had turned a corner and were already heading toward the palace.

"Hey, guys, wait up!" Eric called out. "Guys!"

Thump.

He stopped. He suddenly felt icy cold.

To his right, he glimpsed something in one of those open windows. Red eyes — four of them — flashing in the darkness.

"K-K-Kem?" Eric whispered. "Oh, no. It's Two-head! It's him! It's it! It's . . . oh, help!"

Eric tore off down the street, but some-how — *thump! thump!* — Kem leaped down in front of him, both heads growling.

Then it reared up and jumped at him.

Eric shot around the corner, but his friends weren't there. He must have taken a wrong turn!

Eeoow! Kem howled and thomped even faster after him. Eric dashed around another corner.

Suddenly, he found himself inside a walled garden. It was thick with hanging plants and vines creeping up the walls.

Kem bounded right in after him.

Eric tried to scream, but no sound came out.

Kem slowed, growling under its breath. Step by step it came closer.

Eric looked around. There were hard-shelled fruits about the size of softballs growing on the vines. He tugged one off and threw it at Kem.

Crack! The fruit clattered and broke on the ground. *Plooff!* It gave off a horrible stink.

"Oh, phew!" Eric gasped, staggering back.

The fruit smelled like something rotten. Worse than garbage. *Worse* than worse than garbage!

But Kem kept coming, closer and closer.

With his last ounce of strength, Eric clutched the hanging vines and pulled himself up the wall, tossing more stinky fruits the whole way.

Crack-crack! Plooff!

"Get away, you — thing!" Eric cried.

Then — *krrippp!* — the vines tore away from the wall. Eric slammed to the stony ground.

Kem leaped at him, but the ground gave way and Eric fell *through* it. Down, down, down he went — straight into the open earth.

Five

The Everywhere Passages

Eric slid, rolled, tumbled, then slid some more until — *thwump!* — he hit the bottom.

"Oww!" he groaned. Every part of him ached.

He gazed about, but it was too dark to see. He felt on every side with his hands. There was hard, packed dirt all around.

"I'm in some kind of pit," he mumbled. Looking up, he saw a glimmer of moonlight far away at the top. Very far away.

"Neal! Julie! Keeah!" he cried out.

No answer. Not even the howling and growling of Kem. Eric twisted until he got to his feet. It was hard because the hole was so narrow.

"Galen! Keeah! Help!" he yelled up.

Still, no answer.

Reaching with both arms, he tried to climb, but the sides of the pit were smooth and steep. The more he tried, the faster he slid back down.

"Oh, come on!" he cried. "People! I'm down in this pit! Come and get me —"

"*Spluff . . . muffle . . . pluggh . . . wuff!*"

Eric froze. "Wh-wh-who's there?"

"*Muffle . . . wuggh?*" was the response.

Something was in the pit with him!

Two somethings.

Their noises sounded like words, but of

course they weren't. Then they started scratching.

"They're just digging," Eric said, breathing out slowly. "They won't bother me. They'd better not!"

After a while the sounds died down.

Eric yelled for what seemed like hours.

Why wouldn't they answer? Were they searching Tarkoom for him? What was going on?

Over and over, Eric yelled out his friends' names. His voice became hoarse. His throat hurt.

Finally, he gave up. He hunched up in a ball, tired and achy all over. Exhausted, he fell asleep.

When he woke up, light was streaking across his face. He looked around. Then he looked up.

Droon's sun crossed over the mouth of the pit.

"Holy crow!" he cried. "I've been here all night? Oh, man! Neal! Julie! Keeah! Get me out!"

Still, there was no answer.

Eric felt a sharp pain in his stomach. Hunger.

Of course he was hungry! It had been a day since he'd eaten. His stomach was empty.

Looking up, he tried once more to climb out, but this time he felt something round and hard under his foot.

He reached down and grabbed it.

"Yuck!" he said.

It was one of those smelly fruits he'd found in the garden. Luckily, this one was still in its hard shell. It must have fallen into the pit with him.

He was ready to toss it, when he had an idea.

"The shell is hard and curved," he said

to himself. "If I crack it open, maybe I can use the shell to dig my way out!"

"*Sp-p-pluff . . . m-muffle!*"

Eric laughed. "Prepare to be grossed out, little guys." He took a deep breath, then slammed the shell as hard as he could on the ground.

Crack! The shell split open.

Whoosh! The smell poofed out. It seemed to hit his face directly, like a fist.

"Akkkk!" Eric groaned. In the cramped space, the smell seemed even worse than before.

"*Spliiiifff!*" the creatures cried.

"I agree!" said Eric, pinching his nose tight.

He picked up the broken shell. The fruit inside was dark pink and juicy. He needed to clear it out to use the shell to dig.

He began to pry out the fruit with his fingers.

His stomach ached again suddenly. The hunger was back.

"No way!" he cried. "I'm not going to eat it!"

But he couldn't stop himself.

Slowly, Eric placed a small bit of the fruit in his mouth. Its cool juice swam on his tongue. Holding his breath, he swallowed. Then he breathed again.

He gasped. "What . . ."

The fruit tasted sweet! It was delicious!

"Raspberries!" he said aloud. "That's it. Raspberries, with sugar on top!"

Eric devoured the entire fruit in seconds.

Then he slurped up the extra juice left in the shell. Then he licked every drop from his fingers.

The most amazing thing was that when he breathed again, he no longer smelled the terrible odor of the pod. All he tasted was the wonderful flavor on his tongue.

"This is the most delicious food I've ever eaten!" he cried. "I've never tasted anything so —"

"Please keep it down," whispered a voice.

Eric froze. "W-w-w-what? Who's there?" he stammered.

"You're talking too much," said another voice.

Two pairs of eyes blinked at him from the shadows. They moved into the dim light.

"Whoa!" Eric gasped.

The creatures looked a little like otters. Sleek brown hides covered their short, slender bodies. Their heads were crowned by bright tufts of spiky white fur.

Their eyes were large and round and friendly.

"You're t-t-talking!" Eric said.

"Of course," answered the first. "It's how we communicate. You seem to have learned it, too!"

"But how can I understand you?" Eric asked.

"The tangfruit," said the second. "Its taste is magic. By eating it, you can understand us."

"And in case you couldn't tell," said the first, "you are now speaking our language. The effect will wear off, of course. It always does. By the way, we are called mooples. We live here."

"Pleased to meet you," said Eric. Then a question suddenly exploded in his head. "Wait. If you live here, you must know a way out!"

"A way out of the passages?" said the second. He began to chuckle and snort.

"Where do you want to go? The passages can take you everywhere!"

Eric's heart leaped. "Up there!" He pointed to the top of the pit.

"Just follow us," said the first moople. "Of course, the way in is never the way out. The passages wind and wind. And . . . here we go!"

The two creatures took Eric through a vast maze of holes. Tunnels upon tunnels. Passages leading to other passages, weaving up and around, crisscrossing each other like a pretzel.

"The passages weave throughout all of Droon," said the first. "Under mountains . . ."

"Under castles," said the other. "Volcanoes."

"Underwater?" said Eric as they crawled by a bubbling pool. "Does that lead to the ocean?"

He wondered if the tunnels led to the dark lands of sorcerers . . . and witches.

"The passages lead everywhere!" said the first.

"And they go on forever," said the second.

"They are all over Droon. You may fall in them again sometime," said the first moople.

"And be welcome, too!" added the second.

"As *she* was, poor pretty thing," said the first.

Eric stopped. "There was someone else here?"

"A child. A girl," said the second. "She had such nice manners. Poor thing was lost, I think."

"A girl was lost in the passages?" said Eric.

The first moople scrabbled up through

the dirt. "We tried to help her. Then —
poof! — a big light, and she was gone.
Years ago that was."

The other began to snort again. "Years
ago! That's funny — if you know what I
mean!"

Eric blinked. "Not exactly —"

"You will!" said the first. "And here you
are!" He pointed to an opening above
them. Fresh air poured in. And moonlight.
It was night again.

"Now we must say good-bye," said the
first.

"'Bye. And thank you!" said Eric.

"You are welcome anytime!" said the
other.

The mooples scurried away into the
darkness.

"Strange creatures," Eric muttered. "But
nice."

His arms hurt, his head ached, he was

exhausted, but the smell of fresh air drove him up.

Finally, he slid through the opening. Moonbeams lit an empty street of red cobblestones. Kem was nowhere to be seen.

"Of course not," Eric said to himself. "That was, like, two days ago!"

Eric could hardly believe that after all that time and after all that traveling he was only a few paces away from where he'd started. "Amazing," he mumbled.

He spotted the Tarkoom gate in the distance and went straight for it. Then he heard voices.

He darted into the shadows and peered out.

"He was just here, wasn't he?" said one voice.

"Yeah," said another. "Then he was gone . . ."

Eric's mouth dropped open. It was

Julie and Keeah! And Max and Neal and Batamogi!

"Oh, my gosh!" gasped Eric, staggering over to them. "Guys! Guys! I'm here. You found me!"

"Where did you go?" asked Julie. "We couldn't see you for a minute."

Eric blinked. "For a minute? I was stuck in that pit forever! Then I ate the stinky fruit and now it's tomorrow and — I yelled so much! Why didn't you answer?"

Batamogi and Max looked at each other.

"Eric, you were gone for, like, thirty seconds, tops," said Neal. "What's the big deal?"

"Thirty seconds! It was two days!" Eric said.

Keeah frowned. "No, wait. Something is strange about this. Eric, tell us what you saw."

He told them everything that had happened to him. The creatures he had met. What they told him about the passages. How he wasn't the first one from above to have been there.

"Very strange," said the princess. "I think I've heard about these passages somewhere. Magical tunnels that wind around and around until you get lost in them. And what seems like days there takes no time here."

"Perhaps my master has heard of these passages," said Max. "I wonder if they can help us in our mission to stop Ving."

"Good idea," said Julie. "We'd better catch up to Galen. He went on ahead to find a way into the palace —"

"You there!" snarled a strange voice. "Stop!"

Suddenly — *fwit! fwit!* — the sound of heavy wings filled the air around them.

"Hawk bandits!" cried Batamogi. "Flee! Flee!"

But it was no use. In seconds, all seven travelers were surrounded by an ugly band of bird-headed creatures. They grabbed them with sharp claws and pushed them roughly down the street.

"Bring them to Ving!" one bandit cried, clacking his greasy beak. "He'll be very angry!"

Six

In the Court of Prince Ving

"Let us go!" Keeah cried, trying to get free.

But the bandits only gripped her and the others tighter, dragging them down one cobbled street after another until they reached the palace.

"I hope Galen's okay," Julie whispered to Neal.

Neal nodded. "Maybe he can save us —"

"Silence!" snapped a bandit with a large

stomach and broken wing feathers. He glared at Eric. "You! Tell me where the wizard is."

Before Eric could answer, Max snarled, "We don't know! And we wouldn't tell you if we did!"

"Nice crown you got there!" said a skinny bandit who looked as if he wanted to peck Batamogi to pieces. "Ving will like that!"

"And I like that little morsel!" said the broken-wing bandit, casting his eyes on Snorky, who was shivering in Max's arms.

The kids were pushed from a dark hallway into a huge chamber. In its center stood a colossal stone statue towering up to the high ceiling.

It was a statue of a man with a bird head.

"Ving," snarled Keeah, guessing who it was. "Galen said he loves himself. This proves it."

In the flickering light of a dozen burning torches sat the bandit prince. Ving had a large green bird head and an orange beak that curved down angrily at the tip. Two black eyes the size of baseballs bulged on either side of his face.

From the chest down, except for his feathery arms and his sharp claws, Ving was like a man. He wore armor that was deeply gashed and nicked from many battles.

"Icthos!" Ving called, and the bandit with the broken wing thumped across the floor to him.

Eric tried to hear what they were saying.

"Where is the old wizard?" Ving whispered.

"We did not find him," the bandit told him.

Eric glanced around at the huge room.

He wondered how close Galen was. Was he already planning to rescue them? Had he discovered Ving's plans?

The hawk prince sat up. "Release these people! They are our guests, and free to go!"

"Free to go?" said Keeah as the bandits unhanded her and the others. "But you and your men are thieves and robbers of the worst kind!"

Ving hung his head and sighed, his wings rustling. "That was true once, my dear. But now Tarkoom has risen from its ashes. And we have been given a second chance!"

The words sounded soothing, like a bird cooing softly. Eric felt that Ving might not be as bad as they thought. He *did* say they could go.

"We come back to Droon not to steal again," Ving said softly, almost warbling.

"We welcome this chance to live in peace with all Droonians!"

. . . *And rob Droon's most precious treasure!*

Eric nearly jumped when he heard those words. What? What! He looked around. None of the others seemed to have heard Ving say that.

Ving turned to Batamogi, Max, and Snorky. "Icthos, take your men, and show the Oobja king, the spider troll, and the dog to my room so that they may refresh themselves."

. . . *Put them to work down below!*

Eric gasped. He glanced at the others.

Again, no one had heard the words!

In fact, Batamogi was smiling.

"Thank you, Prince Ving," the Oobja king said. "Perhaps we were mistaken about you. You are welcome in our village anytime!"

Eric couldn't believe his ears. "Wait —" he began, but already the three friends had been whisked from the room.

Ving spoke again in the same soothing tone. "Now, while we await your wizard friend," he said, "how would you like some food?"

Neal slapped his hands together and smiled. "Now, that's more like it. I am so starving!"

"Me, too," said Julie. "And a chance to wash up would be great, too."

. . . Oh, you'll be washed up, all right!

Eric couldn't be quiet any longer. He nudged Princess Keeah. "What's going on here? Don't you hear what he's saying?"

But even Keeah was smiling as Ving went on speaking about the feast he would give them.

. . . Get that wizard once and for all . . . raid everyone's treasures . . . and terrorize

Droon as we did four centuries ago! *Oh, the past shall live!*

Eric listened carefully to the words. It was plain that he was hearing more than the others were hearing. But how could he? Why him?

Then he understood.

"The tangfruit!" he said to himself. In the same way he had heard the furry mooples in the passages, now he understood what Ving was *really* saying. Eric was hearing the truth! The truth behind the lies! And it was all because of the tangfruit!

Keeah stepped forward. "Thank you, Ving. A celebration sounds wonderful. You are kinder than we thought you might be."

Of course! thought Eric. Even Galen had said that Ving had magic in his voice.

Ving bowed his feathery head and

cooed some more. "I am often misunder-stood, I'm afraid."

. . . It is you who will be afraid. . . .

Ving then began to speak to his pirates in a language of clacks and grunts and whistles.

Prepare the bolt. Once these children and their wizard have been taken care of, we will fire the bolt. Then we shall be part of Droon's present. And its greatest trea-sure shall be ours! Go!

Eric's blood ran cold as some bandits bowed, then fluttered out of the chamber.

It will be our biggest theft, he heard them say.

Turning once more to the kids, Ving said, "My dear guests! Go, the party is about to begin. . . ."

. . . For my serpents, who are very hungry . . .

Julie grinned. "I love strawberries!"

"And cookies are one of my essential food groups!" Neal added, nearly jumping up and down with glee. "I can't wait."

Ving smiled. "Then let my men take you . . ."

. . . To the room . . . the floor will give way. . . .

"I hope you find everything to your liking. . . ."

. . . Because no one will ever see you again!

Seven

Room of Tricks

The four children were led away from the giant chamber and into an arched hallway. Eric glanced around for ways to escape, but there were far too many bandits surrounding them.

"Parties are so cool!" said Neal. "Wait until Galen hears where we went! You hungry, Eric?"

"Um, not really," he replied, trying to grin.

Party! Eric knew they weren't going to any party. He just hoped there was a way to escape.

Icthos, the bandit with the broken wing, stopped at a door and inserted a large key. He threw aside the door and waved the children in.

"Right this way for food!" he said, with a clacking sound. Then Eric heard other words.

Food for the serpents — ha-ha!

The bandits pushed the children inside the room and shut the door quickly behind them.

"Okay, so . . . where's the food?" Neal asked.

It was a small chamber. The stone was as red as the rest of the palace, but stained dark. And it smelled damp, as if from water. All of a sudden Eric remembered what Ving had said.

The floor will give way!

"Climb the walls!" Eric yelled.

"Is that where the food is?" Julie asked.

"Do it — now!" said Eric.

The four children squeezed their fingers between the stones and pulled themselves up off the floor. Just in time.

Ka-foom! The floor split in two and fell away.

Splash! Beneath the floor was a pool of black water. The surface broke, and three scaly heads jumped out and snapped at the kids. *Snap!*

"Snakes!" yelled Neal. He kicked one away with his sneaker. "We're not going to *eat* the food. We *are* the food!"

"Now you get it!" said Eric, scrambling up the wall as high as he could go. "Ving tricked you!"

"But Eric, how did you know?" said Keeah, helping Julie climb up next to her.

"The tangfruit," he replied. "Ving tricked you with his weird magic voice. He makes himself sound good. But because I ate that fruit, I heard what he was really saying. And it was all bad."

They climbed halfway up the chamber walls. The serpents leaped up but couldn't reach them.

"Is there a way out of here?" asked Julie.

"Ask them," said Keeah, looking at Eric and pointing to a pair of green-furred mice nibbling crumbs on a row of stones near the ceiling. "Mice always know."

"Plus, the water's getting higher," said Neal.

The water *was* higher. It was splashing at their feet now, and the serpents were snapping again.

Snap! Snap!

Eric pulled himself up the wall. "Excuse

me, mice? I'm Eric Hinkle. These are my friends Keeah, Julie, and Neal. We were wondering —"

"Will you get to the point!" Neal cried.

Eric frowned. "Sorry. Okay, mice, can you tell us how to get out of this room?"

The green mice began to whisper in his ear.

"Uh-huh," said Eric. "Really? Wow. Sure. And then what? Oh. Uh-huh. Really? Okay, thanks."

The mice scampered away into the shadows.

"What did they say?" asked Keeah.

"Well, they've been here for a long time, so they know everything about the whole palace."

Neal nodded quickly. "Yeah, and?"

"And," said Eric glumly, "there's no way out."

"What!" cried Julie.

"No way out," Eric said. "We're doomed."

Neal nearly choked. "D-d-doomed? Oh, man! I'll never see Snorky again —"

"Or Max!" cried Keeah.

"Or Batamogi!" said Julie.

"Sorry," said Eric. "The mice said so —"

Pooomf!

Fireworks exploded in the small room.

Golden sparks showered over the kids and hissed when they hit the cold black water.

And then there was someone with them.

A man. A fairly young man. With a ponytail.

He stood clinging to the wall next to Keeah and Eric. He wore black boots, a long red cape, and a white scarf around his neck. He had a thin mustache and a short beard.

A shimmering, curved staff was slung in his belt. In his hand he held a short, glowing stick.

He grinned when he saw the kids. "Hi! Need some rescuing?" He pointed the glowing stick at the water. "Wand, send those serpents home!"

Zzzzz! A spray of sparks sizzled into the water. The serpents jumped and snapped once, then vanished into the depths below.

The black pool went still.

"That was awesome!" said Julie.

"That?" the man laughed a cheery laugh, tucking the wand in his belt. "It was nothing!"

"Wow, thanks, whoever you are," said Neal. "But, I mean, like . . . who *are* you?"

The man smiled. "People call me Shortbeard."

"*Short* . . . beard?" said Keeah, searching his face carefully. "You look a little familiar. . . ."

"But you can call me Galen," he added.

The princess gasped. "But it can't be!"

"But it is!" said the man. "Don't you like it?"

Eric's mouth dropped open. All at once, he, too, saw something familiar about the man.

They all saw it.

"Holy crow!" Julie said. "You *are* Galen! You were here when Tarkoom was destroyed four hundred years ago! And now you're here with us! So you're you! You're *young* Galen!"

The young man gave them all a quizzical look. "If you say so . . ."

Then, as quickly as they could, and all talking over one another, the four children explained how Tarkoom had appeared in modern-day Droon, how Galen was now four hundred years older, and why they had come to Tarkoom.

"If we don't stop Ving from changing Droon," said Keeah, "Tarkoom will stay. And Ving and his evil bandits will return to our time."

"You don't want that, believe me," said Galen. "But I just got here myself. I don't know what dastardly deed Ving is planning."

Eric frowned. "I heard him telling his bandits to prepare the bolt. Whatever that means."

Galen chewed his lip and shrugged at the same time. "Bolt, huh? Well, there are good bolts and bad bolts. There's a *bolt* of cloth. That's good. But I don't figure Ving is thinking about a change of clothes."

"Probably not," said Neal. "He's got all those feathers already."

"Right," said Galen. "Then there's a *bolt*

on a door. Could be that. Bolt also means to run fast. But that doesn't sound right, either. . . ."

Keeah and Julie gave each other a look.

"Plus, we have to rescue my dog," said Neal. "And Max and Batamogi, too."

"Ving sent them down below," said Eric.

"Then we need to split up!" said Galen, aiming his wand at the wall. He muttered a word and — *poomf!* — sparks shot everywhere. When the smoke cleared, there was a hole in the wall.

Galen bounded out to a high corridor.

"I'll head to the throne room. Ving is sure to be there," he said. Then he pointed down a shadowy hallway. "The stairs are that way. That's probably where they took your friends."

"I'll go," said Neal. "I hope Snorky is okay."

"I'll go with you," said Julie, smiling at Neal.

"Meet us in the throne room as soon as you can," said the young wizard. "We'll be teaching Ving not to mess with the good guys. And be careful!"

Julie and Neal snuck off into the darkness.

"We need to be careful, too," said Keeah. "We don't want to meet up with any bandits —"

"Ha! I eat bandits for breakfast!" Galen boomed. "Now, come on!" Then he grabbed Eric and Keeah by the hand and shot away down the hall.

Eight

The Bad Kind of Bolt!

The kids ran through the hallways, following Galen's flying cape and glowing wand.

"You're fast!" said Keeah, running to keep up.

"Not bad for a hundred and forty-two, eh?" Galen said, laughing. "Boy, I love this!"

Eric nearly laughed, too. It was funny to think that the old Galen they knew so well had been such a wild adventurer when he was young.

Suddenly, they heard clacking noises. They slowed down.

Before them stood the giant throne chamber.

Eric peered in. "The place is crawling with bandits," he said. "I don't see Ving, though."

But there was something else to see.

A round stone platform was rising up slowly through the floor.

On it stood something big and ugly.

A giant crossbow.

Eric had seen pictures of such things in history books. A bow was attached to a long, straight shaft. A thick cord was stretched far back and locked into place. But this had to be the biggest crossbow ever made. It was as big as a house.

And sitting on the shaft, poised and ready, was an arrow as long as a flagpole. At its tip was a jagged sliver of gold that spat and sizzled with what seemed like electricity.

"My gosh!" whispered Keeah. "I've never seen anything like that. It looks like a lightning bolt!"

"It is a lightning bolt," said Galen, his eyes darting around the room.

Eric slapped his head. "Of course! Lightning bolt! That's the kind of bolt Ving meant! And it's huge. But how will he steal treasure with that?"

"Let's not wait to find out," said Keeah.

When the crossbow was in place next to Ving's statue, six large bandits tugged on a large wheel at the base of the bow. The wheel turned.

As it did, the bow's shaft began to lift.

At the same time, the room's ceiling was gradually pulling apart to show the countryside around the Panjibarrh Valley.

"There is the Oobja village!" shouted one of the bandits. "Aim the bolt right at it! Hurry!"

Eric squinted to see, then his mouth dropped open. "It's Batamogi's village in the dust hills! They're going to fire this huge arrow at it!"

"There must be treasure buried under the mountain," young Galen whispered. "That's what Ving is after."

Keeah turned to them. "We can't let this happen. If that arrow destroys the poor village, it will change Droon forever!"

"It won't happen," Eric said, turning to the princess. "We won't let it."

Galen nodded quickly. "You bet we won't. I won't let these bandits escape into your world."

He pulled the curved staff from his belt. It was made of wood but glimmered with many colors as he swung it back and forth in the hallway.

"Cool," said Eric.

"My rainbow cutlass," said Galen. "I invented it myself. It'll make sure those bad guys never get a chance to use that bolt!"

Keeah glanced across the room. "Eric and I will take care of that big ugly crossbow."

"I like the way you think," said Galen. "All we need now is the element of surprise —"

"There they are!" snarled a bandit from inside the room. "By the door! Three of them!"

"Forget the surprise — let's go!" said Galen. With a single swift move, he jumped into the room, his cutlass whistling and sending off streamers of sparks.

The kids jumped in after him, running for the crossbow, but two bandits swept up into the air and swooped at them, their beaks clacking.

"No you don't!" Keeah said. She skidded to a stop and shot her hands out. "I'll stop you —"

Kkkk — blam! One red ball of sparks and one blue one blasted from her hands. They exploded together in a cloud of purple smoke!

The winged men fell to the floor, coughing.

"What was that?" said Eric, scrambling over to Keeah.

"Um . . . wizard *and* witch powers, I think," she said, blowing on her sparking fingertips. "It would be nice if I could control them!"

Fwing! Clang!

The wizard flicked his cutlass quickly and sent three more bandits spinning high into the air.

When they stopped spinning, they were too dizzy to fly. They fell to the floor — *thud-thud-thud!* — their eyes rolling around in their heads.

"Not so hawkeyed now, are you?" Galen said with a grin.

"YOU!" boomed a voice from behind them. "You will not laugh for long, wizard!"

The three friends whirled around.

It was Ving himself! He flew into the room, his black eyes blazing with anger. He thrust out his claws so fast they seemed to blur in the air.

"We don't need any tangfruit to understand you now, Ving!" said Keeah.

"Puny humans!" said Ving. "You will not stop me! My lightning bolt can destroy whole mountains. It shall destroy the Oobja village, too."

"The furry little guys make you mad or something?" Galen asked, whirling his glittering cutlass around in the air.

"Under their mountain is what I seek most!" Ving snarled. "The royal tombs of ancient Goll!"

The sly smile dropped from Galen's face. "But opening those tombs will release the old dark magic! You can't do that!"

"Watch me!" snarled Ving.

"No, you watch me!" Galen boomed. He whacked at Ving with his glittering cutlass.

Ving dodged the blow and lunged at the wizard with his claws outstretched. "Let the battle begin!"

Instantly, Galen and Ving pounced on each other, and — *clang-a-clang!* — the battle had begun!

Nine

Wild, Wild Droon!

Kwish! Fzz-ang! The large chamber echoed with the clashing of claw on cutlass as Ving and Galen fought.

In the confusion, five bandits jumped to the crossbow and began turning its heavy wheel.

Errck! Errck!

"The village is in our sights," Icthos called out.

"Fire when ready!" Ving shouted back as he lunged at Galen.

"Never!" cried Keeah. She shot a blue burst of light, and Icthos and the other bandits jumped away from the giant bow.

Eric ran with her across the room. They climbed up to the bow. "Let's aim it somewhere else," he said. "So Droon won't be changed."

"Good idea!" said Keeah. She and Eric gripped the wheel.

Kwish! Ving soared over Galen, flashing his claws at him from above. "Give up, wizard!"

"Keep your claws to yourself!" Galen replied. With a snap of his fingers, he soared to the top of the statue and landed on the giant stone head.

Glong! Clank! Across the statue's giant head, over the shoulders, down the arms, and back up again, the wizard and the bandit struggled.

"It's no good!" Eric cried, pulling on the heavy wheel with all his strength. "It won't budge!"

"Fire the bolt!" Ving shouted. Icthos scrabbled back to the bow. He began climbing up.

"Time for some special magic," said Keeah, her eyes taking on a strange look. Eric wasn't sure what it meant. Then she said, "Touch my hand. I think this will work. We can both turn that wheel."

"But it took five hawk men to move it!" Eric protested.

Keeah smiled at Eric. "We can do this. I'm sure we can. If I don't fry us both, I mean. . . ."

Eric blinked at his friend. Then he knew what she meant.

Keeah had begun to master her *other* powers.

When Eric touched her hand, he felt his arms tingle, first with cold, then with heat. Finally, he felt himself surge with strength. "Whoa! I feel really strong!"

Together, they gripped the giant wheel.

Errck! It began to turn. As it did, the shaft moved until it pointed nearly straight up.

"We're doing it!" Keeah said. "Keep turning."

"I'll stop you!" came a snarly voice.

It was Icthos! He had scrambled up behind Eric and Keeah. He reached for the firing lever.

"Fire the bolt!" Ving cried again.

"No!" Eric cried. He and Keeah turned the wheel once more as Ichtos pulled the lever.

Fwung — zwing! The bolt shot straight

up, like a long, flaming sword, right through the open ceiling and straight into the night sky.

"Yes!" cried Eric. "It's going off course! Batamogi's village is safe! Ving won't change Droon!"

Ving shrieked at the sight of the arrow flying harmlessly into space. He turned to the children.

"Bandits!" he howled. "Destroy them!"

"Not so fast!" came a yell from the hallway. It was Julie. She rushed in with Batamogi, Max, and Snorky. Three bandits swooped at them.

"I'll stop those nasties!" Max chittered. He spun a web of spider silk and flung it over the bandits' wings. They tumbled to the floor.

"And I'll finish the job!" Batamogi cried. He tossed a tangfruit at them and jumped away.

Crack! The hard shell broke on the floor, and the bandits ran out into the hall away from the smell.

From atop the statue, Ving trembled with rage. His black eyes narrowed at Keeah. "Old Goll *will* live again. And to make sure of it — I will destroy *you!*"

With one sudden move, Ving struck at Galen, then swooped at Keeah, his claws aimed like daggers.

"Keeah!" cried Eric. "Watch out —"

All of a sudden —

Poomf! Fireworks exploded in the room, light flashed, Ving was hurled to the floor, and a cloud of blue smoke covered everything.

A figure in a long blue cloak jumped from the smoke. He thrust both arms at Ving, his fingertips sizzling with sparks. It was old Galen!

"Begone, fiend, or you shall know what magic really is!" the old wizard boomed. "Goll shall remain in the past — and so shall you!"

Ving sputtered and snarled and clacked his beak in anger. But it was clear that Galen was ready to strike with all his might.

"You have not seen the last of me, old man!" the hawk bandit yowled. Then he picked himself up off the floor and jumped, and soared into the corridor after his bandits.

"Galen!" cried Keeah, hugging the old wizard.

"Hey, that's my name!" said the young Galen.

The old wizard turned to the young one. A smile crept over his lips.

"Well, well," he said. "Look at you!"

The two wizards studied each other closely.

Young Galen frowned and scratched his short beard. "Strange. You're actually me, aren't you?"

"Rather, you . . . are me!" said the old wizard, tugging on his long beard.

"This is weird and a half," mumbled Eric.

"You can double that," Julie added.

"I would," said Eric, "except there are too many doubles in this room already!"

Finally, the young wizard grinned a big grin and shook hands with his older self. "This is quite strange, even for Droon. But it's nice to meet you, old man!"

"Too bad we must leave now," old Galen said.

"Must we?" asked Keeah. "It's fun just

watching the two of you! The stories you could tell!"

"We must," old Galen said. "Because of that!" He pointed up through the open ceiling.

They could see that Ving's lightning bolt had flown straight up, blazing into the night sky, and was now starting to come back down again.

"It's heading right for Tarkoom," said Julie.

"Correction," said Max. "Right for the palace!"

"Right for where we're standing!" said Keeah.

"We'd better bolt!" young Galen cried. "Before that bolt blasts us! Come on, everybody!"

Eric started to run, then stopped. "Wait. Where's Neal?"

"Oh, dear!" said Max, trembling as he looked around. "We must have lost him in the halls. Poor Neal, I hope the bandits didn't catch him!"

Eric gasped. "We have to find him! We have to —"

Ka — boom!

The sizzling lightning bolt hit the palace.

It blew apart the giant statue of Ving and blasted a huge crater into the floor. Rocks and dust and flames exploded everywhere.

Suddenly, Snorky raced out of the chamber, barking and yelping just like he had that morning when Neal was chasing him. *"Woof! Woof!"*

"Snorky!" cried Eric. "Wait! Not you, too!"

But flames roared all around the room,

rising higher and higher. Smoke filled the air.

The earth trembled and quaked.

And the vast city of Tarkoom began to fall.

Ten

Friends, Friends, Friends!

Fwoosh! Boom! Flaming stones crashed down from the walls. Fire poured out through the hallways and corridors. The city of red stone turned into a city of red flame.

"We must leave before the city is destroyed!" said Galen, pulling everyone into a corner away from the fire. "We must go now!"

"We can't go without Neal!" cried Eric.

Then, there he was.

Out of the smoke, Neal stumbled into the throne room. Snorky was nipping at his shoes to keep him moving. Everyone rushed to him.

Neal grinned as Snorky jumped into his arms and started licking his face. "He fetched me!" Neal said. "He actually fetched me! Finally, I have a real pet!"

"Excellent!" said the younger wizard. "Now we can all get out of here. Follow me!"

"No," the older Galen said. "We must go separate ways. You to the past, we to the present."

The young man looked at the older, and nodded slowly. "So . . . I guess this is good-bye?"

Old Galen smiled. "It is. But remember,

while your world has dark days now, they will pass. You must always believe in Droon. And love it."

"I will," his younger self replied firmly. "I mean, seeing you and these kids, I guess I always did believe. I mean, you did —"

"We both did, and do," said Galen Longbeard. "Now go to the storeroom. You will find a flying carpet. You must escape Tarkoom, or I would not be here. But be careful. There's danger."

The younger wizard grinned, his eyes twinkling in the light of the flames. "Danger? Old fellow, you just said the magic word!"

"You and your wild, wild ways!" old Galen said. "Now I know why my hair turned white!"

With that, Galen Shortbeard dashed recklessly across the burning room and into the hallway.

"He was so cool," said Neal. "I mean, *you* were cool, Galen. I mean, you still are —"

Just then — *eeeoow!* — a familiar howling echoed through the halls of the burning palace.

"Kem!" said Julie. "We forgot about him. He sounds mad that we busted up his city."

"We need to get out of here," said Eric. "And I know just the way. The passages!"

"Quickly, everyone," said Keeah. "Fast, fast!"

Eric led them all through the burning halls and corridors of the palace until he came to the garden.

"In the ground," Eric said. "Into the tunnels!"

They all piled into the hole he had fallen into earlier. Eric heard the furry mooples digging far away. He started for the sounds, worming his way through the dark passages.

Suddenly, Keeah tugged on Eric's sleeve. "Excuse me, Eric. This is the wrong way," she whispered. She looked at a tunnel on her left. "We need to go this way!"

"But . . . how do you know?" Eric asked.

Keeah blinked, then said, "I just know." She began climbing through the narrow tunnel. It turned upward. Soon they felt cool air wafting over them.

"I knew it," said Keeah softly.

Suddenly, Eric knew it, too.

Keeah had been in the passages before.

She was the lost little girl the mooples had told him about. She was the girl with nice manners.

Yes, it all made sense now.

It was in the passages, somewhere,

sometime, that Keeah and Witch Demither had met.

It was where Keeah got her witch powers.

Eric knew it, though he couldn't prove it.

And maybe it was in the passages — the passages that went everywhere — that Keeah somehow came to the Upper World. To his world.

Eric knew it all. He would find some way to tell Keeah. He would tell her. He had to. Soon.

"I see stars!" cried Batamogi. "Home! Home!"

They scrambled upward, and the cool air of the valley rushed over them.

Julie was the first one out, helping Max, Neal, and Snorky. Galen and Batamogi were next.

As his friends worked their way out of the passage and into the fresh night air of Droon, Eric paused.

He waited alone in the passage and listened.

He heard the voices of the friendly mooples cheering for them. He also heard sounds from everywhere the passages led to. He heard the washing of waves on a distant shore, the roar of flames, the singing of children in Jaffa City.

He heard the cry of the wind, of ice creaking in the frosty north, the hooting of birds in faraway forests, and the babbling languages of hundreds of different peoples and creatures from all across Droon.

"The everywhere passages," he said to himself. Then, as he climbed up through the hole and into the valley, he slipped onto his side.

And he hiccuped.

"Hic!"

And it all went silent.

The noises, the voices, the sounds.

All were gone.

The tangfruit's gift had worn off.

"Come on," said Keeah, taking him by the hand and pulling him up. "And look at this!"

Behind them, the city of Tarkoom shimmered in the flames. The fire roared higher and higher.

Just then, Galen Shortbeard, perched on a small flying carpet, soared up over the smoke.

"He escaped!" said Max. "I like that boy!"

"He is unharmed, as are the bandits," old Galen said with a smile at his younger self. "They are just being sent back to their own time."

"And out of ours, thank you!" said Keeah.

As they watched, the scene before them shimmered once and faded. Young Galen vanished, and with him went Tarkoom, Ving, his hawk bandits, and the ancient past itself. The valley became still.

Once again, the honey-colored columns were tumbled and silent. The red walls were fallen.

And the great statue of Ving was no more than a mound of dust, blown smaller and smaller with each new breeze from the Panjibarrh hills.

Eeoow! The howling of Kem echoed across the night. It grew more and more distant.

"He got away!" said Eric, looking out over the purple valley. "Where do you think he'll go?"

Galen gazed into the west. "Probably to

find his first master. The one who created him."

"Who's that?" asked Julie.

"Ah!" the wizard said, still scanning the horizon. "You know him all too well. He is Lord Sparr."

Keeah gasped. They all did when they heard the sorcerer's name.

"I knew we hadn't seen the last of him," said Neal. "Even his name gives me the creeps!"

Suddenly, the air brightened behind them.

"The stairs have appeared," said Batamogi. "The Upper World calls the children back."

The small band of friends made their way over the silent plains to where the magical stairs stood shimmering on a hill.

"You have done good work today," Galen told Eric and his friends. "As always, we could not have done this without you. Now, Keeah, without delay, we must find Kem. Find Kem, and we shall find Lord Sparr!"

Keeah looked at Eric, Julie, and Neal. Then she shrugged. "Well, life in Droon is never dull!"

With a final wave to the kids, Galen, Keeah, Batamogi, and Max started across the plains and back to camp.

Eric turned to his friends. "Was that the coolest adventure ever?"

Neal grinned. "Absolutely. Until the next one!"

"We'd better get going," said Julie. "We have a kitchen to clean up. And a living room. And a dining room —"

"Thanks to Snorky," said Neal. He glanced around. "Oh, no, where's Snorky? Snorky!"

The dog came prancing over to the

stairs, licking his whiskers. His paws were stained with bright pink juice.

Eric gasped. "Uh-oh! Snorky ate a tangfruit!"

"It probably won't hurt him," said Julie.

Snorky licked his whiskers again. "Hurt me? It was delicious! But I want to go home now."

Neal's mouth dropped wide open. "Snorky . . . ?"

Snorky trotted up the magic staircase.

"Hmm," he said. "I wonder if humans can learn to fetch cookies. . . ."

The three friends stared at one another.

Then they all raced up the stairs for home.

Under the Serpent Sea

And again to Dolores,
who makes the fantasy real

One

A Mystery Dream

"Kkkk! Boom-ba-boom!"

Eric Hinkle was jumping on his bed and making noises.

"Ka-blamma-bam!"

His friends Julie and Neal were watching him. Julie's mouth was hanging open. Neal's eyes were as big as moons.

"My dream started with a *huge* storm!" Eric said, waving his arms. "Thunder was pounding the house. Rain was coming down in buckets!"

He paused to catch his breath.

Neal gulped. "Don't stop now, man. Tell us everything you saw."

Eric swallowed once and went on. "It could be a dream about Droon," he said, lowering his voice to a whisper. "But the next part is sort of a mystery. You have to tell me what you think."

Julie and Neal both nodded silently.

Droon.

They would never forget the day they discovered the entrance to the magical land of Droon.

First they found a door hidden by some old crates and cartons in Eric's basement.

Then they pulled the door open and piled into a small closet. The next thing they knew — *whoosh!* — the floor vanished and they were standing on a shimmering staircase.

The staircase led down to a strange and wonderful world. In that world, the good wizard Galen and the young princess Keeah battled a nasty sorcerer named Lord Sparr and a mysterious sea witch called Demither.

Since their first adventure, Princess Keeah had become one of their best friends. Sometimes she would send them a magical message asking them to come. At other times the kids would know through their dreams about Droon that Keeah needed them.

"I hope you did dream of Droon," said Julie. "It's been weeks, and I want to go back."

But Eric's latest dream wasn't like any other he'd ever had. It was more like something that had really happened.

"I was small, maybe four years old," Eric began. "The storm was scaring me, so I went to the basement to hide."

"When I'm really afraid, I sort of freak out," said Neal. "I hide my head and hug my blanket, or maybe a pillow —"

"Neal, *shhh*!" said Julie. "Eric, go on."

Eric tried to remember everything. He closed his eyes. Yes, it was coming back to him. . . .

"It was dark in the basement. . . ." he began.

Rain was splashing against the window over the workbench. The apple trees outside whipped around in the wind.

Suddenly — *boom!* — there was a big banging sound. And the closet door burst open!

Bright red light filled the basement.

"I dived behind an old chair!" Eric said.

"Then, right before my eyes, two people stepped out of the closet and into the room."

"Yikes!" Neal gasped. "Who were they?"

Eric told them what he had seen.

One of the figures was a child about his age, dressed all in blue. The other was a grown-up who wore a long dark cloak.

"*What is this place?*" the child said. It was a girl's voice. "*Are we still in Droon?*"

"*No,*" said the tall one in a voice like a woman's, but very deep and scary. "*Come, we must do this quickly or he will find us.*"

"*The big bad man?*" asked the girl.

"*Yes,*" said the woman. "*I gave you the red light to help you escape him. And I will give you more. But first, follow me.*"

"The girl might be Princess Keeah," said Julie.

"Then the big bad man would have to

be Lord Sparr," said Neal. "He's the biggest, baddest man in Droon. But keep going, keep going!"

Eric told them how, in no time, the two strangers were across the basement floor and up the steps. They moved swiftly, as if their feet didn't even touch the floor.

Quietly, carefully, Eric followed them.

The two figures swept up the steps and into the dark living room. They fluttered past the sofa, the coffee table, and the television.

They started up the stairs to the second floor, then up to the attic.

"There was a weird glow under the woman's cloak," Eric told his friends. "She was hiding something, but I couldn't tell what it was."

"So you followed them to the attic," said Neal, reaching for Eric's pillow. "Then what?"

Eric told how he saw the two figures standing under the sloped roof. Before them was a large window looking out the side of the house.

"*I want to go home,*" the girl said, trembling.

"*Soon,*" the woman answered. "*We must do this together. Are you ready?*"

"*Yes.*" The girl held out her hands.

"*This will be the last time,*" the woman said. "*Then you will have my power.*" She touched the girl's hands.

Zzzz! — a bright red light passed between them, then stopped. The girl held up her hands.

"*I have it now,*" she said.

Red sparks shot from her fingertips.

Eric gasped, and the woman turned sharply, showing her face for the first time. Her features were twisted. Her skin was rough and scaly.

"Hurry! Open the window!" she snapped.

The girl moved her hand and, as if by magic, the window sprang open. Cold wind and rain rushed into the attic.

Without another word, both figures spread their arms, ran to the window, and leaped out.

"They flew!" said Eric, bouncing on his bed again. "Over the trees and high over the street. It was so awesome! I think they dipped behind the library, but the storm got too wild to see. Finally, I woke up." He sat down on the edge of the bed. "So what do you think?"

"Whoa," Neal murmured. "I love the flying part. I wonder what it's like having cool powers like that. Not that we'll ever know. . . ."

Julie's eyes shone. "If the girl was

Keeah, I think we're being called back. I think we should go!"

She and Neal jumped to the bedroom door.

But Eric didn't move.

"What's the matter?" asked Neal.

Eric frowned. "Well, our dreams usually come true in Droon. But I was *little* in my dream. So was Keeah. This dream can't come true."

"But what if it's not really a dream?" said Julie, suddenly excited. "What if it's a memory? I mean, maybe it actually *did* happen. And your dream is what you re-member —"

Eric stood up. "Of course! I can't believe I didn't think of it. Remember when Keeah said she had been in my basement once be-fore? But nobody could figure out how?"

"Galen and everybody said it was im-possible," said Neal.

"Well, maybe it's not so impossible," said Eric. "If my dream really did happen, it proves that Keeah *was* here before!"

The three friends stared at one another.

They were all thinking the same thing.

They needed to get to Droon right away.

In no time they tramped down the stairs to the basement. They began pulling away the cartons blocking the closet door under the stairs.

"But if the girl was Keeah," said Neal, "then the other person was . . ."

Eric shuddered, remembering the woman's strange face. "That voice, the scaly skin. I know who it was. It was Demither. The witch."

They all shivered to think of her.

The witch had a history of doing bad things. Once she transformed into a giant sea serpent and destroyed Keeah's ship.

Another time, she tried to kidnap Keeah's mother, Queen Relna.

"If it was Demither," said Julie, "it would explain how Keeah seems to have witch powers."

"Exactly," said Eric. "Wizard powers give off a blue light. But Keeah also had red powers like Demither. They're sort of wild and dangerous."

"But why were the two of them in your house?" asked Neal. "That's the biggest puzzle."

"And maybe we'll find out today," said Julie.

The kids piled into the closet. Eric closed the door behind them and Neal switched off the light. The room was dark. Then it wasn't.

Whoosh! The floor vanished and they stood at the top of a rainbow-colored staircase.

Together, the three friends descended the stairs. Down they went through a layer of wispy clouds. Below them, the bright orange sun of Droon shone on a magnificent city.

"It's Jaffa City," said Neal. "Right on Keeah's doorstep. We're pretty good at this, you know?"

Eric grinned at his friends. "Yeah, we are."

But as they hurried down the stairs, a sharp wind rose up and nearly blew them off the side.

"Holy cow!" said Julie, struggling to hold on.

Then hard, icy rain began pelting them.

Before they knew it, large black clouds swept across the sky, completely blotting out the sun.

"What's happening?" asked Eric.

"I don't know, but I see Galen's tower,"

said Julie, pointing to a tall tower standing near the city walls. "Let's try to get over there now!"

"Right," said Neal as the sky boomed with thunder. "Maybe Galen has a blanket I can hide under. This is getting scary!"

Two

Day of Night

The kids ran breathlessly from the stairs all the way to the upper room of Galen's magical tower.

Entering, they screeched to a halt.

"And I thought the weather outside was bad," gasped Eric, looking around the room. "There's a snowstorm in here!"

It did look like a snowstorm.

A snowstorm of paper.

Galen, the white-bearded wizard, was making papers fly all over the cluttered room.

"Now where is that prophecy?" he bellowed, snatching at papers, then sending them off again. "Max! Bring Quill! Keeah! Bring my mirror!"

"Um . . . Galen?" said Julie. "Hello. . . ."

The wizard turned and blinked. "Ah, children! This is a black day for Droon. I must discover where this queer storm is coming from. Max! Where are you? And where is *Quill*?"

Scritch-itch! A sharp scratching sound came from across the room.

Galen whirled on his heels. "There you are!"

Max, the wizard's eight-legged spider troll helper, staggered in under the weight of an enormous book. Standing upright in the book was a long, curved feather pen named Quill.

The kids had seen Quill before. He was a magical pen who wrote down everything that happened in Droon. Sometimes he wrote so fast, he wrote the future. He was writing quickly now.

"Hello, friends!" Max chirped, setting the fat book on Galen's table. "I certainly hope Quill can help us get to the bottom of this storm —"

"Oof! Oh, help! Mirror . . . heavy!" groaned a muffled voice behind the children. They turned to see a big silver mirror edging its way into the room. Someone was under it, trying to carry it.

"It's Keeah!" said Julie.

The kids rushed to the princess, helping her set the mirror down in the center of the room.

Keeah smiled. "Thank you!" she said.

When Eric saw Keeah's light blue tunic, he was more convinced than ever that she was the girl in his dream.

"How did you know to come?" she asked.

Neal was so excited he just blurted it out. "Eric dreamed about you! About when you came to the Upper World! With Demither! The witch!"

Instantly, all the papers fluttered to the floor, Keeah's mouth dropped open, and Max fell over.

Galen frowned. "Eric, tell us everything."

Eric took a deep breath and described each detail of his dream. By the time he'd finished, everyone was staring at him.

"We all think it really happened," said Julie.

Keeah turned to Galen. "I remember

being in Eric's basement, but not the rest of it. And *not* the witch!"

The wizard stroked his snow-white beard slowly. "Clearly, Demither gave you some powers, powers that you cannot control yet. That fire at breakfast this morning, for instance. Or the snakes in my silver washbasin . . ."

Keeah frowned. "I'm sorry about that," she said. "I don't know how any of that happened."

"Exactly the reason we must be careful," said Galen. "Though why the witch gave you powers at all is still the most puzzling of puzzles. I only wish you remembered more of it —"

Kkkkk! A jagged bolt of lightning flashed outside the tower's windows, illuminating the black sky.

"But I see we have more pressing concerns!" Galen said. "Mirror — awake! Show me where this storm comes from."

Zzzzt! There was a loud buzzing sound, and the gray surface of the old mirror cleared.

It showed a rocky coast whipped by rain and wind. Just beyond the jagged cliffs a dark sea was spinning into an enormous swirl of water.

"A hurricane," said Julie. "A big one."

"That must be the center of the storm," said Eric. "But what's out there?"

"More like *who's* out there," said Max, his orange hair standing on end. "That is the Serpent Sea, off the coast of Mintar. Known as the home of Witch Demither!"

Keeah peered into the mirror. "Do you think she's *causing* the storm? But how . . . and why?"

Scritch! Scratch! The magic feather pen suddenly began writing in the book.

"Ah!" said the wizard. "Quill will tell us all!"

The feather pen whizzed furiously across two full pages, then stopped. It seemed to Eric that the pen breathed heavily, and then lay down on the book to take a nap.

Galen read the pages. His face turned pale.

"Master, what's wrong?" asked Max.

The wizard shook his head. "Quill says this storm is indeed the work of Demither —"

"I knew it!" chirped Max. "It's some evil new plan to make the good people of Droon suffer!"

"But there is more," said Galen quietly. "Quill writes that Demither is using the Red Eye of Dawn to cause this storm."

"Oh, man, does it get any worse?" Neal groaned.

The Red Eye of Dawn was a magic jewel created by Lord Sparr to control the forces of nature.

He was planning to use the Eye to help him conquer all of Droon for himself. Then Witch Demither stole the Eye from him.

Now she was using it to make the storm.

Boom-ba-boom! Thunder rumbled overhead, shaking the tower from top to bottom.

"It feels like the end of the world," said Julie, shivering. "What can we do?"

All eyes turned to Galen.

"It is quite clear what you must do," he said. "You must go to Demither's realm under the Serpent Sea of Mintar. There you must stop her from using the Red Eye. Steal it from her if you have to."

Keeah turned to her friends. "Mintar is on the far side of Droon. Will you come with me?"

Eric nodded. "I think that's why we're here!"

"Good," she said with a smile. "Luckily, Friddle the inventor has set up his workshop nearby. He'll help us get to Demither's lair. Follow me!"

She marched quickly out the door.

As Eric, Julie, and Neal went to follow her, Galen raised his hand. "A moment please, my friends. I must tell you of something else that Quill wrote. A warning."

Eric shot a look at Neal and Julie.

"What kind of warning?" he asked.

Galen read from the book. "Quill writes that Keeah will undergo a dangerous trial today. Her powers will be tested as never before. If Keeah fails her trial, it could mean doom for her."

"What kind of trial?" Eric asked.

"What kind of *doom*?" asked Neal.

Galen scratched his brow and went on. "Every young wizard is tested to see if they are worthy of their power. Unfortunately, Keeah possesses not only the good wizard arts but also the angry red arts of the witch. If she becomes afraid or angry, her powers may overwhelm her."

"If that happens," said Julie, "does it mean she might never become a real wizard?"

"Or worse," Galen replied. "The dark powers might turn her against us. And against Droon."

The three friends stared at one another.

"What can we do to help?" asked Eric.

"Alas," said Galen, "Quill warns us not to tell Keeah about this. It might only make matters worse. Also, since I myself would be tempted to help Keeah, I cannot go with you."

"You're not coming?" Julie said. "We're going to the witch's house and you won't be there?"

The wizard gave a half smile. "Perhaps I can find a way around that. Now go stop Demither from using the Eye. And stay close to Keeah."

"We'll stick to her like cheese on a pizza," said Neal. "You can count on us."

"Same here," said Eric. "What Neal said."

The three kids ran down through the tower. When they popped out below, Max was there.

"Children!" he chirped. "Do not let my master join you on your mission today. Quill says he may not."

"I think we'd notice him," said Julie.

"Ah, but Galen is tricky!" said Max. "He is a wizard, after all. He may not look like himself."

"You mean he'd come in disguise?" said Neal. "Like with blue eyebrows? Or big clown feet? Or a bald head? Or the ultimate disguise, glasses?"

Max blinked at Neal. "Just so. But if you see him, bop him right on the nose! He hates that."

"Bop him?" asked Julie. "Bop Galen's nose?"

"What if it's a fake nose?" asked Neal.

"Either way!" Max said. "If he meddles with the prophecy, it may mean *doom* for Keeah!"

Neal grumbled, "There's that word again."

Three

Fasten Your Sea Belts!

Blam! Zzzz! Plink!

Strange noises were coming from a small hut at the edge of the forest just outside the city.

Eric, Julie, and Neal rushed to join Keeah at the tiny door. It creaked as they opened it. *Errrch!*

Inside the hut, they found a short man whose friendly smile, thick glasses, and very large ears they had seen before.

It was Droon's master inventor, Friddle.

He bowed to them. "Welcome, all of you!"

As tall as Galen's tower was, the inventor's workshop was long and low. It was filled from wall to wall with odd devices and contraptions.

Neal's eyes lit up, and he began touching everything. "This is the awesomest cool stuff!"

"The ultimate workshop," Eric agreed.

"Friddle, we're on a mission," said Keeah. "We need to get to the coast of Mintar."

"Oh, dear!" said the inventor, running his hands through his fuzzy green hair. "To Witch Demither's underwater realm, eh? You'll need something to get you down to her secret palace."

"And back up again, right?" asked Julie.

"Most definitely," said Friddle.

"What's this thing?" Eric asked, pointing to a thick belt with several compartments on it.

"Ah, I call it my sea belt," the inventor said. "The green button helps you dive. The yellow button brings you to the surface — Neal?"

From the worktable, Neal had picked up a pair of big round glasses. "Wow! These make everything magically blurry. What are they?"

Friddle frowned. "My extra pair of glasses! Now pay attention, please. Each of you must take a sea belt. But whatever you do, don't touch the red button on the belt."

"Why not?" asked Neal, picking up a belt and tapping lightly on the red button.

"Never mind!" said Friddle sharply. "It's not perfected yet, so don't try it. Now follow me!"

Whoosh! Icy wet wind blew into the workshop as Friddle opened the tiny back door.

Outside the hut stood a large bulky shape covered completely by a huge brown cloth.

"What's under there?" asked Keeah.

"Oh, wait till you see!" said Friddle, tugging the cloth until it billowed to the ground.

He beamed. "I present . . . my Flying Flapper!"

What sat before them was a plane. But it was unlike any plane the kids had seen before.

Two thin, rounded wings were attached to each side of a long skinny frame. Five cushioned seats were set inside from front to back. And a big wooden propeller stuck out of the flat nose.

Julie jumped with excitement. "It looks

just like a big bug. It reminds me of a dragonfly!"

Friddle giggled at Julie. "What a mar-
velous name! *Dragonfly* it is. It flies by yip-
yip power!"

He tapped a round cage at the front of
the plane. In the box were two large balls
of blue fur.

Keeah peered closer at the fur balls.
"Yip-yips? Why do you call them —"

"Yip! Yip!" cried the creatures loudly.
"Yip!"

The princess laughed. "Never mind."

The moment the blue fur balls awoke,
they began running in their cage. When
they did, the propeller on the plane's front
began to turn.

Friddle climbed into the pilot's seat.
"Hop aboard the *Dragonfly*, adventurers!"

The four friends piled in, Friddle pulled

levers and pushed buttons, and — *yip-yip-yip!* — the plane shot forward.

It bounced roughly along the ground as the double sets of wings flapped wildly. The instant they lifted off, the storm spun dark air around the plane. Swirling mist covered everything.

"The storm is fierce," said Friddle nervously. "I can't see where we are! What's ahead?"

"I see something," said Neal. "It's . . . it's . . . yikes! A tree! A big one! We're going to hit it!"

Suddenly, a blast of red light shot from Keeah's hands and the tree burst into flames and crashed straight to the ground.

The plane cleared it easily.

"Oh, dear!" Keeah cried. Instantly, she muttered words under her breath. A spiral of blue light swept over the fallen tree and set it upright again, its leaves greener than before.

"I'm so sorry!" she said. "Oh, what would my mother think of me having such powers!"

"The queen would be very proud," said Friddle, pulling the plane up from the city. "For one thing, you are quite brave to make this journey!"

Keeah's mother, Queen Relna, was one of Droon's greatest wizards. But she was under a terrible spell, cursed to change into one animal after another. Most recently she was a dolphin.

Eric gazed at Keeah. He wondered if her mother had been tested as she was going to be. He wished he could tell her what Galen had said about the trial she was going to endure.

But maybe the wizard was right.

Keeah's powers *were* very sensitive.

Besides, if someone did try to help her, they might only make things worse. No, the best thing was to stick close to her, as Neal had said.

Like cheese on a pizza.

For the next two hours the plane soared over Droon. Through the storm they spotted the frosty Ice Hills of Tarabat, the lush Bangledorn Forest, and the rolling deserts of Lumpland.

Suddenly Friddle slapped his hands together in glee. "Ah! Going into Demither's mysterious realm! The danger! The excitement! The danger!"

"Um . . . you said *danger* twice," said Neal.

"There'll be plenty to spare!" said Friddle.

At that moment, they flew over the jagged cliffs of Mintar.

"My gosh," Keeah murmured. "There it is!"

A black tower of wind and water roared up from the green sea, swirling the waves and spinning dark clouds all around it.

"The center of the storm!" said Friddle. "Now remember what I told you about your sea belts. I've brought some helmets for you, too. With them, you'll be able to breathe and talk underwater. When I fly close, you jump out and dive into the water. If I am right, you will find Demither's lair right under the hurricane!"

As they tightened their belts and donned their helmets, Neal laughed nervously. "I never expected to go skydiving in scuba gear. I hope everything works right."

Eric was about to respond when he spotted something on the horizon. "What's that?"

Darkness was spilling up over the edge of the sea, turning the waves from green to black.

"Holy cow," said Julie, squinting. "It's . . . ships. Hundreds and hundreds of ships. Black ones. And they're coming this way."

"Who would be crazy enough to be out in this hurricane?" asked Neal. "Besides us, I mean."

"Whoever it is, you must hurry!" Friddle shouted. "The hurricane is growing stronger. My poor wings are being torn apart. And the yip-yips are getting tired. You must jump now!"

"Then let's go!" said Keeah.

Climbing out onto the tail of the

Dragonfly, the four friends held hands tightly.

The plane dipped into the swirling tower of wind and water.

The kids shut their eyes.

And they jumped.

Four

Into the Creepy Deep

"Ahhhh!"

They all screamed at the top of their lungs.

But their cries were lost in the winds spinning inside the hurricane. They hit the water hard.

Splash-splash-splash-splash!

"Try to stay together!" Eric cried out.

"Good luck!" shouted Neal. "Someone pulled the plug! We're going down!"

And down they went, into the churning waters of the Serpent Sea. Bubbles rushed around them, and strong currents spun them faster and faster.

Pressing the green buttons on their belts steadied them. They drifted down quickly and soon hit the bottom. *Thud-thud-thud-thud*.

Far above them, the ocean's surface swirled angrily from the hurricane. Down below, the water was calmer. It rippled with soft green light.

Gangly plants quivered and waved at them.

"Is everyone okay?" Julie called. Her voice carried through the water to the other helmets.

Eric scrambled up next to Neal, a thin stream of bubbles floating up from his helmet. "All in one piece," he said.

"Then let's get going," said Keeah. "We

have to find Demither's palace. And we don't have much time —"

Rrrr! Just then the ground rumbled, red light flashed through the water, and the storm above spun even faster.

"Demither's playing games," said Julie.

"Well, she'd better not win!" said Neal, gulping loudly inside his helmet as they pressed on in search of Demither's lair.

The first thing they came upon was the wreck of a giant ship. Seaweed sprouted from the deck. Fish swam in and out of the cracks in its hull.

"Many ships have met their doom in Demither's waters," said Keeah. "I'll take a look."

She swam away to the front of the ship.

"Met their *doom?*" said Neal. "I'm really getting to not like that word —"

"Neal, don't freak out," said Eric. "It's scary, sure. But we need to help Keeah. She's the one on trial, remember. So let's stick together."

"Together, huh?" said Neal. "Where's Julie?"

Eric looked around. Julie was nowhere to be found. "Julie —"

"Oh!" came a cry from behind them.

They spun around to see Julie disappearing into the ship, a long tentacle coiled around her.

"Something's got her!" cried Neal.

They swam over as fast as they could. Inside the wreck Julie was cornered by a long snakey creature with fins all over its head. Two eyes burned fiercely on either side of a red snout.

It let Julie go when Eric and Neal barged in.

All of a sudden, bubbles spurted from Julie's air tube. She was laughing inside her helmet.

Then she swatted the monster's red nose.

"Eerrgh!" The creature let out a loud cry, then slithered away into the shadows.

Neal gasped. "Whoa! That was either the bravest thing in the world or the dumbest! That was one ugly sea monster!"

Julie laughed again. "That was no sea monster. It was Galen! Did you see that fake red nose? Max said to bop Galen if we saw him. So I did!"

"Yeah, but are you sure it was —" Eric began.

Kkkk-kkk! Light flashed again, sending strong shock waves through the ship.

An instant later, Keeah was there. "I found something you have to see," she said. "Hurry!"

They followed Keeah over a range of hills jutting up from the ocean floor.

Then they saw it.

A giant dome of rippling green glass.

It spread for miles across the ocean floor.

"It sure is big," said Julie.

Inside the dome were giant sea caves, buildings made of red coral and blue stone, and long, curving bridges of shiny white shells.

"I think we found Demither's lair," said Eric.

"No," said Neal, "it just found us!"

The water sizzled with electricity, and suddenly sea creatures appeared on every side of them.

They looked like sharks except that they had many legs and two sharp tails curling up behind them. Moving swiftly, the creatures coiled a chain of spiky sea-weed around the children.

"We're trapped," said Julie. "Should we fight?"

Keeah's fingers lit up with red sparks. Then she shook her head. "We could. But maybe we want to be captured. If these are Demither's guards, they could lead us to her."

Eric was relieved not to fight the creatures.

"Keeah's right," he said. "The sooner we find Demither, the sooner we get out of here and back on dry land."

"I like that idea," said Neal.

The princess put down her hands.

As she did, a pair of giant rocks nearby split open to reveal a dark watery cave. The creatures' noises made it clear what the children should do.

"I guess we go in the cave," said Keeah.

"I guess we do," said Eric.

The creatures tugged on the chain of seaweed, and the children entered the cave. The walls inside were carved here and there with scenes of a terrible sea serpent attacking ships.

"They call Demither the serpent queen," Julie mumbled. "Now I see why. She rules this place."

Neal nodded. "The first time we saw her, she was a sort of mermaid. The next time she was a serpent. I sure hope she's being her mermaid self today, because her serpent self scares me!"

The twin-tailed creatures led them through the cave and into the green dome itself.

The kids swam up into a pool and stepped out onto a stone plaza. The floor around them was inlaid with rich green and blue tiles and golden stones. Looking up, Eric saw the hurricane still whirling fiercely above them.

"We can take off our helmets here," said Keeah. "There's air."

The kids removed their helmets and hooked them to their belts.

From inside, the dome looked like a big glass bowl turned upside down. In its center stood a palace of emerald-green glass. Five stone towers surrounded the palace, their tops made of spiraling shells.

In every free spot, lush seaweed gardens grew wildly. Pools and fountains bubbled everywhere. And instead of streets, blue-water canals meandered slowly toward the central palace.

The sea creatures ushered the kids across the square and into the green palace. Inside was a throne room unlike any other that they had seen.

The throne itself was a giant scallop shell. Its top was open and curved over a silvery pool.

On each side of the throne were urns blazing with green flames that leaped and fell when the children entered.

The sea beasts removed the chain binding the kids, then slid over to the pool and waited by it.

"Nice place for a not-nice person," Julie whispered. "I wonder what she'll do with us."

Suddenly there was a splash in the pool and something slithered out onto the throne.

It had the head and arms of a woman, but the scaly tail of a fish. She might have looked like a mermaid, except for her rough face and cold expression.

"It's her!" Eric whispered.

It was her. The sea witch. Demither.

"So . . . you have come to my world," the witch said in a raspy voice. "I knew my hurricane would attract your attention."

Eric was sure he'd heard that voice before.

In the dream that was more than a dream.

In Demither's hand was a long staff with an iron claw at its head. In the grip of the claw was a bright crimson stone.

"The Red Eye of Dawn," said Demither, thrusting the staff into a holder by her throne.

At those words, a bolt of sizzling flame burst from the red jewel and crackled over their heads.

"Yes!" said the witch. "The Red Eye of Dawn is alive — and it is angry!"

Five

Black Fire, White Wings

Keeah stepped toward the witch's throne. She narrowed her eyes and spoke.

"Demither, you must stop this storm. We will take the Red Eye of Dawn if we have to —"

"Take the jewel," said the witch softly. "I only wish you could. . . ."

Keeah blinked. "Uh . . . excuse me?"

The witch raised her sunken eyes to the children. She looked different from the last time they'd seen her. She had once seemed very powerful. But now her skin, usually sea green in color, looked almost yellow. Her lips were thin and pale.

"She seems . . . sick," whispered Eric.

"The Red Eye of Dawn has done this to me," Demither said. "It will do it to you, too."

Keeah glanced at her friends, then back at the witch. "What do you mean?"

In the pale light of the green fire, Demither began. "Sparr created this red jewel. I stole it, hoping to gain more power. Ha! Only then did I discover the evil spirit who dwells in the Eye. A spirit more terrifying than I ever imagined."

The children looked at one another.

Keeah said nothing.

"What kind of spirit?" Julie asked finally.

"His name is Om," said the witch.

"Lord Sparr conjured him long ago to destroy whoever possesses the jewel. Even now, Om is draining my power from me. And the Eye grows stronger."

Neal nudged Julie. "It's true," he said softly. "She doesn't look too good."

The jewel pulsed slowly with light.

"See," said the witch. "Even in his sleep, Om listens to his evil master . . . Sparr."

"But Sparr vanished," said Eric. "We heard he almost died. No one has seen him for months."

That was true. The sorcerer had been hurt by another of his terrible creations, the Golden Wasp. After that, he had simply disappeared.

"When the Wasp attacked him, Sparr was changed, perhaps forever," the witch replied, drawing slow breaths. "Not even I know what he looks like now. But he is alive. And he is coming for the Eye."

"Let me guess," said Julie. "He wants the Eye so he can try to take over Droon again."

The witch nodded slowly. "That is why I have used my magic to conjure the Doom Gate."

Neal squeaked. "Is doom, like, *everybody's* favorite word? What's a Doom Gate, anyway?"

"An enchanted prison," said Demither. "Once the Eye is sealed inside it, it can never again be used for evil."

"Evil?" Keeah snapped. "You're a fine one to talk. For all we know, this is a trap that you and Sparr set to capture us!"

Demither narrowed her eyes at the princess. "You do not know me!" she snarled. "It was I who shared my power with you. It was I who stole the Eye from Sparr, stopping his plans to conquer Droon. Yes, and it was *I* who told you your mother was alive!"

"*Then why didn't you stop Sparr from cursing her?*" Keeah said, her fingertips sparking.

"Keeah!" said Eric. "Your powers —"

"Because!" said the witch. "Sparr did not curse your mother — *I did!*"

Keeah gasped sharply and staggered back.

"You . . . you?"

"See for yourself what happened that day at Sparr's fortress," said Demither. "Watch and learn what befell your queen!"

The witch waved her hand and a whooshing sound came from the pool beneath her.

An instant later the pool went still. On its surface was the image of Queen Relna. She was dressed in silver robes and flying on a carpet over Sparr's black fortress.

Suddenly the sorcerer swooped in from nowhere, his cloak flapping like wings, the jagged fins behind his ears purple with rage.

"Queen of Droon!" Sparr yelled. "I have you now! Prepare to end your days!"

Relna swerved, but Sparr was too quick. He hurled a bolt of black fire at her.

Zzz — blam! Relna fell back and Sparr zoomed in, shrieking with mad laughter. "I have won!"

All of a sudden, the lake exploded.

Out of it burst the head of a giant serpent.

It was Demither!

"You will not harm her!" the witch boomed.

"Go back under the sea where you belong!" Sparr bellowed.

Blam! He shot a second fiery bolt at Queen Relna. She was thrown from her carpet and fell lifeless through the sky.

"Mother!" Keeah winced, watching the scene through her parted fingers.

But from Demither's eyes came a piercing red light. It surrounded the queen and slowed her fall. A moment later, the light vanished and something white fluttered up into the air.

A bird.

"The white falcon!" Keeah gasped. "That's how my mother became the falcon. You put a spell on her!"

In a final angry move, Sparr hurled a bolt of sizzling black fire at Demither. She took the blow in her heart and shrank back into the lake.

The scene blurred and vanished, and then the pool was just a pool again.

Keeah watched the water until there was nothing more to see. She stood there stunned, unable to speak. Finally, she turned to Demither.

"You saved my mother's life," she said softly. "You didn't have to, but you did. Why?"

Water splashed suddenly behind them.

"Demither saved me," said a voice, "because . . . she is my sister!"

Everyone turned. There, bobbing up from the depths of another pool was a sleek black dolphin.

They all knew who it was.

It was Queen Relna.

Six

The Puzzle's Pieces

Keeah ran to the pool, knelt, and hugged the dolphin. "Mother, Mother! Is it true?"

The queen nuzzled her daughter. "Yes, my love, it is true. Demither and I are sisters."

Keeah stared at her mother. "But how . . . why didn't you ever tell me?"

"I forbade her to tell you until you

needed to know," Demither said. "My story is a sad one."

Julie turned to Eric and Neal. "Talk about a day of surprises!"

Neal blinked. "So Witch Demither is now . . . *Aunt* Demither? That's fairly weird."

"Keeah, my love," said the dolphin queen, "long ago my sister and I shared the same powers, the same love of Droon. But she . . ."

Relna stopped, struggling to find the words.

"I chose the way of strength over that of family," Demither hissed from her throne. "Sparr offered me greater powers. I followed him. But I grew greedy. You see what has become of me. Now Sparr is coming here to reclaim the Red Eye once and for all —"

At that moment, a rumbling sound echoed into the dome. Everyone looked up to see a shadow spreading over the surface of the sea.

"The black ships," said Julie. "They're nearly here."

"It is Sparr's warriors, coming for the Eye," said Demither. "Alas, Om has made me weak. Now only Keeah has the power to seal the jewel in Doom Gate."

Keeah looked at her mother, then at the witch. "Me? What do you mean? Why me?"

Demither dived into the silver pool, then surfaced, her skin even paler than before.

"Wizardry alone cannot stop Sparr," she replied. "His magic is deeper, darker, *older* than Galen's. Seven years ago, Keeah, I told your mother this. She did not believe me. So I took you and fled through the tunnels that weave through Droon's underground —"

"The passages!" Eric gasped. "Of course! They connect every place to every other place. I fell into them once."

"It was in the passages that I gave you my powers," Demither said to the princess. "I knew you would need them to fight Sparr one day. But first you needed them for a dangerous journey."

"To the Upper World!" Neal blurted out. "Just like Eric remembered in his dream!"

"But why?" Keeah demanded of the witch. "*Why* did you take me to the Upper World? What was the dangerous journey? Tell me!"

Crash! Clang! Darkness swept over the dome.

The black ships were directly over the palace.

And the green water outside was turning red.

Red . . . with Ninns!

Hundreds of Lord Sparr's red-faced warriors were jumping into the water. They were riding fierce, dragon-tailed fish with spiky teeth and bulging yellow eyes. They dived swiftly to the palace.

"Ninns *plus* sea monsters!" cried Neal. "It just doesn't get any worse!"

Demither's eyes flashed. "They have come for the red jewel. Keeah, you alone, using all your powers together, can seal the Eye away from Sparr."

"But how will we get in the Doom Gate?" Keeah asked.

"You yourself are the key!" the witch said. "You will find the Gate in a grotto beneath this palace. In the Gate are three rooms. In the final chamber is a pit. You must seal the Eye in that pit. And remember — just as power can be shared, it can also be stolen. Be wary of Om. He is dangerous —"

Crash! The Ninns, with helmets looking like goldfish bowls on their heads, burst into the throne room. Water splashed wildly around them as they rushed in.

Keeah grasped the staff. Red light sizzled down the length of the staff to her hand.

She winced, but did not let go.

"Keeah, be strong," said her mother. Then she turned to Demither. "Sister, I will help you!"

"Get the Eye!" the Ninns grunted.

"No!" Relna declared. "Sparr will never get his hands on the jewel!"

"Take it, Keeah!" cried Demither. "Go now!"

As Ninn arrows whizzed into the throne room, the kids slipped away to the

narrow, twisting tunnels below the palace. Deeper and deeper they went, the light dimming around them, the sounds of fighting growing distant.

Finally the tunnels ended, opening into a large room carved from the jagged rock under the palace.

"This must be the grotto," said Keeah softly, trying to peer into the darkness.

With her friends close beside her, the princess grasped the staff tightly and stepped into the cave. When she did, a silvery glow lit up the darkness.

And they saw it.

"Whoa, it's big," said Neal with a low whistle.

Eric swallowed loudly.

"I think we found the Doom Gate."

Seven

The Gate Called Doom

The Doom Gate was a huge slab of stone. It stretched like a wall from the grotto floor to the high ceiling above.

A black door was set deep into the bottom of the Gate. In its center was a flat space in the shape of a hand.

"That must be the first of the three doors," said Eric. "We enter the Gate there."

"And you are the key," said Julie, re-membering Demither's words.

"Then come on," the princess said. "Let's all stick together."

Eric smiled. "Like cheese on a pizza," he whispered to himself.

Keeah placed her hand flat against the center of the door.

Kkk! Boom — boom! The black door slid aside with a thunderous sound. Be-yond it stood a smaller room carved from the rock around it.

But the instant they entered the room, the door clanged shut behind them.

"It's a trap!" said Julie, suddenly afraid. "I told you we shouldn't have gone in —"

Neal gave her a look. "No, you didn't."

Julie frowned. "Well, I was thinking it!"

"It's all right," said the princess, looking around. "Demither conjured the Doom

Gate to keep people out. I guess we should think of this as a sort of trial."

"A trial?" said Eric, glancing quickly at Julie and Neal. "I guess you could call it that."

He wondered if Keeah had any idea that she herself was being tested. She seemed brave and strong, but with so much magic in her, who could tell what would happen?

Especially in a place called Doom!

In the red light of the flickering Eye, they saw that the rocky room was very cold. Ice had formed all the way up the walls. A path winding to a second door across the room was matted with frost. Clusters of icicles hung from the ceiling.

"Well, we found Demither's freezer," said Neal, shivering. "But I don't think we'll find any ice cream."

Sssss! A hissing sound echoed off the walls.

"What was that?" Eric asked.

Keeah nodded. "I heard it, too."

Spar-r-r-r!

It was raspy and low. But whether it was more like an old man's voice, or like a whispering child's, Eric couldn't tell.

"Who said that?" said Julie, looking around.

The red jewel flared and sizzled in the staff.

Then they knew.

It was Om, the spirit in the stone.

Sparr made me. Demither stole me. You shall free me!

"Whoa, a jewel that talks," said Neal. "Well, think again, Eyeball. We're not freeing you. We're here to put you in your place!"

Are you him?

Neal blinked at the jewel. "Him who?"

No, it's not you. It's the other. The quiet one.

"Hey, is there an off switch on this thing?" Neal asked, backing onto the path. "Because he's starting to scare me —"

"Neal!" Julie cried. "Watch out!"

Suddenly — *crack! whoosh!* — a long, sharp icicle broke off from the ceiling and fell at Neal. Then another fell and another. He tried to jump away, but there was nowhere for him to go.

"Helllllllp!" he screamed.

Keeah thrust out her hands and — *zzzing!* Red light surrounded Neal. He flailed his arms and legs for an instant. Then — *ploomf!* — Neal was no longer Neal.

He was a turtle.

A baby sea turtle.

Crash! Crunch! Crack!

The icicles shattered on Neal's hard shell, sprinkling icy dust harmlessly across the floor.

Julie snatched Neal from the ground. "Keeah, you saved him! That was amazing!"

"Amazing?" Neal squeaked. "Amazing? It's terrible! Now I'm just like Queen Relna! I'll go from shape to shape. A chipmunk. An elephant. A worm! None of my clothes will fit —"

"Please don't freak out," said Eric.

"Neal, I'm sorry," said Keeah, touching his shell lightly. "I'm not sure where that spell came from. I know I can change you back, but not right now. We need to keep going."

Clang! Crash! The sounds of the battle in the palace echoed down into the cavern.

"And we need to go fast," said Eric.

"Wait here." Keeah held her hand up over her head and flicked her fingers. A shower of silver crystals fell over her, the flakes plinking and tinkling together like hundreds of tiny bells.

"What's that for?" Julie asked.

"Just watch," the princess said. She gazed up at the ceiling. "Here I go!"

There was a blur and a sudden whizzing sound where Keeah was. Then she was gone.

"Where did she go?" Neal started.

The next instant — *fwoosh!* — she was on the other side of the chamber, smiling brightly.

Then — *thwack! flang! crunch!* — every icicle fell from the ceiling and crashed to the floor right where Keeah had been just seconds earlier!

Eric blinked. "That was so cool!"

"It's safe for you to cross now," Keeah said.

Julie popped Neal into a small pouch on her belt, and she and Eric ran to the princess.

Keeah set her hand on the second door and it slid aside like the first.

But this time the room ahead was a warm green garden full of strange and beautiful plants.

"This looks much better," said Eric. "I think."

They stepped in carefully, Keeah in the lead.

"What's going on?" Neal asked in a squeaky voice, peering out of the pouch. "Anything happening?"

Just wait! hissed Om's voice.

Suddenly one of the plants nearest Eric unfurled two spiky tendrils and grabbed for him.

"Veggies!" cried Eric. "With attitude!"

He managed to dodge out of the way when the plant lunged. But Julie wasn't so lucky. The spiky shoots wrapped around her arms and yanked her off her feet.

"Ohhh!" she cried. The plant tightened its grip and twisted her upside down, sending Neal clattering to the floor.

Keeah jumped for the plant, muttering words in a language Eric had never heard before.

A red light covered Julie. She shuddered once, then — *poof!* — became a snake.

"A fire snake!" Keeah announced, surprised. "I didn't know I could do that, either."

Julie slithered easily from the plant's grasp. Then she turned and breathed on the plant.

Tssst! A blast of hot air withered the tendrils.

"Serves them right!" said Neal, snapping the toasted tendrils off with his beak. "Yum!"

Clang! Clonk! More sounds of fighting echoed into the Doom Gate.

"We'd better keep going," said Keeah. "Julie?"

"Spicy breath at your service!" Julie said. She slithered across the floor, burning a path of roasted plants to the far end of the room.

Eric wondered if Keeah's trial was going well. With two of his best friends turned into strange animals, he wasn't really sure.

He picked up Neal and popped him into the pouch on his belt. Then he tapped Keeah's arm.

"You can change Julie and Neal back, right?" he whispered. "Because I'm pretty sure their parents will be mad if I bring back a turtle and a snake instead of them."

"Of course!" Keeah said confidently. Then she whispered, "I hope so, anyway."

With that, she placed her hand on the final lock, the door slid aside with a *boom*, and they headed together into the last chamber.

Eight

The Spirit in the Stone

The innermost chamber of the Doom Gate was shrouded in shadows.

"Am I still in my shell?" asked Neal, poking his head out of Eric's pouch. "Or is this room dark?"

"It's-s-s dark," Julie hissed, coiling near Keeah's feet.

With a whispered word, the princess opened her palm, and a ball of blue wizard light rolled from her hand.

"Wizard powers are still the best," she said.

She tossed the ball high, lighting the chamber.

Right away, the light began to fade.

"There is magic in this place," Keeah said.

Eric peered into the gloom.

The chamber was almost perfectly round. A narrow stone bridge led from the door to a sort of island in the center. On either side of the bridge the ground fell away to nothing.

"I don't like it here," said Neal. "It makes me want to hide my head."

"Stay here, all of you," said Keeah. With the staff grasped firmly in her hand, she stepped onto the bridge. The others stayed near the door.

"This place makes me feel creepy," said Julie. "And for a s-s-snake, that's s-s-saying a lot!"

Eric felt it, too.

There was something frightening about this final chamber. He hoped Keeah wasn't as afraid as he and his friends were. It might mess up her powers just when she needed them most.

He watched Keeah closely.

As she crossed the bridge, a strange hot wind began swirling around the walls of the room.

It was coming from the staff. From Om.

"There's a pit in the center of the island," Keeah called. "And an iron lid that seals shut. That's where Om needs to go."

Eric hoped Keeah would be able to do it.

But Om didn't want to be inside the pit.

The closer Keeah drew to the pit, the fiercer were the sparks shooting off the end of the staff.

Flashes of red flame darted out of the

gem, circling the room and crackling overhead. The hot wind howled even louder.

Om was angry.

Eric stood by the door as Neal pulled
his head into his shell and Julie curled up
next to him.

"This is it," Eric murmured, watching
Keeah. "This is her trial. And we can't help
her. . . ."

On the island now, Keeah lifted the
staff over her head. Then she turned the
staff down toward the dark pit.

"Good-bye, Om," Keeah said. "The Red
Eye goes dark . . . now!"

Noooo! Om howled. *Keeah! Look . . .
look!*

The staff began to shake in her hands.

Eric tried to see what was happening,
but the storm grew louder and darker and
fiercer.

Keeah — look! Om whispered.

Suddenly there were castles forming out of the swirling wind, and piles of gold, and armies of warriors as far as the eye could see.

Use your witch power to set me free, Om shouted. *All this will be yours. Yes! Then I will share my power with you!*

"Or steal mine from me — like you stole Witch Demither's!" Keeah snapped.

You are part witch now!

"Begone, Om!" she cried. "Into the pit!"

Nooooo! Om shouted.

At once, the red storm swept around her.

"Keeah!" said Eric. He knew he wasn't supposed to help her. But he couldn't stop himself.

"Keeah!" he shouted. "Keeah!"

Eric battled the winds on the bridge. He

made his way across and leaped onto the island. Struggling to help Keeah, he, too, grasped the witch's staff.

You! Om shouted at him. *You!*

The staff felt strange in his hand. As if it were water running through his palm.

Hot water. Very hot!

Then he knew what it was. It was *power.*

"Owww!" cried Eric. "It's burning me!"

You are him, aren't you?

"What?" said Eric.

"I didn't say anything," said Keeah.

"Om did!" said Eric. "He's trying to scare me!"

Suddenly Om sent a blast of red light out from the Eye. The explosion struck Keeah and knocked her far from the pit.

She tumbled off the island.

"Keeah!" Eric cried.

Great howling noises filled the chamber. Wind tore at Eric. The island rumbled and shook.

"Keeah!" he called out. There was no answer.

A huge flame burst from the gem angrily and whirled around Eric as he clutched the staff.

You saw where they hid it.

"Keep quiet!" snapped Eric.

They, the princess and the witch. They hid it in your world. Seven years ago. You will find it.

"I don't think so!" Eric shouted angrily.

You will find it and bring it . . . to Sparr!

Eric's arms suddenly felt as heavy as stone. His head ached. He wanted to sleep. He felt weak all over. Just as Demither had felt weak.

He closed his eyes.

He felt his grip on the staff loosening.

Then he was falling . . . falling . . .

He dropped the staff . . . and fell off the island.

"Eric!" cried a familiar voice.

Suddenly Keeah was there.

Her long hair flying back, her face red from the heat of Om's anger, Keeah grabbed the staff.

Then she shot a beam of light at Eric.

He stopped falling.

The light flowed over him, flashing from her fingertips and into him. It was not the red light of witches that flowed over him.

It was the blue light of wizards.

The light surrounded Eric, and he felt suddenly strong. He flew up from the darkness as if by his own power.

He jumped back onto the island.

Together he and Keeah clutched the staff tight and, with one mighty thrust, they threw it deep into the pit.

Noooo! Om howled.

Red fire leaped out of the pit. But a bright blue burst of light forced it back.

Then, with a loud and final *wump!* Keeah kicked the thick black lid over the pit.

Instantly, the storm vanished. Om went silent. The Red Eye went dark. The chamber was still.

Eric looked over at the princess. His knees felt as if they were made of jelly.

She stared down at the pit and tried to catch her breath. Finally she spoke. "Well, that was something."

Eric laughed. It was strange to hear himself laugh, but that was all he could do. "That was something, all right! You did it!"

"No," she said. "We did it. Together. I just hope I didn't hurt you with that blast of light."

Eric shook his head. "Actually, it felt great!"

Together they walked back over the

bridge to Neal and Julie, who lay fast asleep near the door.

Keeah closed her eyes, her face going still. "Okay, then," she said. Murmuring some strange words, she held her hands over them.

A moment later — *poof!* — Neal and Julie were not only awake, they were themselves again.

"Did anything happen?" asked Neal, stretching his neck.

Eric shot a smile at Keeah. "Not too much."

"Then we'd better get back to the dome," said Julie, doing a little wiggle. "My snake hearing was telling me that the fighting is worse."

As they headed back through the door, Eric turned one last time. The dark lid over the pit glowed for an instant, as if it were red-hot.

And he thought he heard Om whisper once more before the chamber went black.

"Eric, come on," said Keeah. "Our battle isn't over yet."

Eric turned from the chamber and trotted over to her. As he did, a smile broke out on his face. Keeah had won at least one battle right there. The wizard in her had won out over the witch.

Keeah had passed her trial.

"Come on," he said. "Let's boot those Ninns back where they came from. No jewel for them. They're going home empty-handed!"

"Yahoo!" Neal yelled. "Now you're talking!"

"Let's go!" cried Julie.

Nine

Ninns in the Grotto

Cheering loudly, the four friends raced back through the three doors of the Doom Gate.

They charged out into the big grotto.

And stopped dead.

"Uh-oh," muttered Neal. "Talk about battles not over yet . . ."

Om's rumbling and storming had cracked the walls of the grotto. Water was rushing in from outside. A whole ocean of water.

So were Ninns, hundreds of them, riding in on their sharp-toothed fish monsters. The spiky tails on each fish whipped about wildly as the waves washed them in.

"Helmets on," said Eric. "We're going underwater!"

There was a dull *thunk* as the first Ninn arrow struck the Doom Gate behind their heads.

"Don't those Ninns have anything better to do than attack us?" Julie asked.

"Attack them!" bellowed the chief Ninn.

"Guess not!" said Keeah. "I'll just have to stop them the old-fashioned way. With a spell."

She raised her hands and flicked her fingers at the charging Ninns.

Fzzz. A tiny spray of blue sparks left her fingers, traveled a few inches in the air, sputtered, then faded.

Neal was nodding slowly as he watched the Ninns advance. "Okay. Now really do it."

Keeah's eyes grew big. "I can't. My battle with Om must have weakened me."

Neal was still nodding. "Then could I be a turtle again? *Because I need somewhere to hide!*"

The Ninns surrounded them on every side and began pushing them back against the Gate.

"Now what do we do?" asked Eric.

"I know what I'm going to do," said Neal. "I'm going to freak out. I've been holding off because the timing wasn't right. But now I'm going to freak out and I don't care who sees it!"

Eric saw Neal's finger go for his belt. "Neal — don't! Remember what Friddle said —"

Neal pressed the red button on his sea belt.

Whoomf! A tiny jet of flame burst suddenly from the back of Neal's sea belt.

"Whoa — it's hot!" he cried. Before he had a chance to say anything else, he blasted straight through the front line of Ninns.

Flimp! Bloink! Ooof! Yeowwww!

Screaming, Neal whizzed around the grotto at lightning speed, leaving a trail of foamy water and toppled Ninns behind him.

"Help!" he cried as he zipped by his friends. "Can't control it — *glub!* — need — help!"

He blasted through another bunch of Ninns and zoomed up the tunnel to the throne room.

"Well, he freaked out," said Julie. "But he escaped."

"We need to get out of here, too," said Keeah.

"Too late for that!" growled a deep voice.

A rush of bubbles burst in their faces, and three fat Ninns charged in on their fierce sea beasts.

"Get the princess!" the Ninns grunted.

"Never!" said a familiar voice.

Suddenly — *thwump!* — the Ninns and their creatures went crashing into the grotto wall as a smooth black shape swam out of nowhere.

It was a dolphin!

"Mother!" Keeah exclaimed, rushing to her.

The Ninns shouted and grumbled inside their fishbowl helmets. But they sped off quickly.

"Follow me," the dolphin queen said. "Demither needs us, all of us."

With a wiggle of her flippers, Relna motioned for Keeah to climb onto her long, sleek back. "Let's go!"

Speeding ahead, Relna bumped Ninns out of the way, clearing a path for Eric and Julie.

Eric looked at his friend. "Well, should we freak out, too?"

Julie grinned. "It's the only way!"

They both hit the red buttons on their belts.

Whoomf-whoomf!

They shot across the grotto after Keeah and her mother. Together they rocketed up through the water-filled tunnels and finally back into Demither's throne room, where they met up with Neal.

Ker-splash! Eric and Julie broke through

the water's surface and shot straight up to the dome.

"How — do — we — stop?" Julie cried.

"Try — pressing — the — button — again!" shouted Neal, who was still zooming around.

They all pressed the red button a second time.

The three friends smashed against the inside of the dome — *splat!* — their jets died — *fzzzzt!* — they plummeted straight to the ground and dropped right into Demither's pool — *splash!*

When they jumped to their feet they saw that Demither's guards had pushed the Ninns from the throne room.

But that wasn't the biggest news.

The biggest news was Demither.

She was turning into a sea monster.

Ten

The Wizard Queen

Demither's tail, now long and spiky, splashed wildly in the pool beneath the throne.

Her eyes, sunken before, were now gleaming red. Her skin was turning crusty and covered with spikes.

Claws were growing where fingers had been.

"Sparr is casting his spell over me once

more," the witch said. "He is near — so near!"

"We will help you," said Relna.

"There is no time," Demither replied. "Keeah, come to me quickly. Together we will release the queen from her spell."

Keeah looked at her mother.

"You must trust her," said Relna.

Wump! Wump! The Ninns were using pieces of the wrecked ship to batter on the dome.

Keeah took Demither's hand.

Kkkkk! Blue light from the princess mixed with the red light of the witch and became a shimmering purple. Then the light flowed outward to the dolphin, swirling around it.

As the light encircled the queen, Relna's black skin turned ashen, then as bright as sunlight. Then the dolphin vanished.

"But where — " Keeah said.

A moment later — *slooosh!* — there was a sudden spray of crystal water. A fountain of light and air and wind filled the dome.

When it cleared, Relna stood before them, a queen once more.

"She's beautiful!" gasped Julie.

Relna was dressed in a long wizard's cloak. It was all pearly white and stitched with glittering quarter-moons of gold and blue.

Around her head sat a crown of diamonds.

Even though her eyes told of many years of trial and heartache, she beamed at her daughter.

"Mother!" said Keeah, running into her arms. "I've waited so long for you!"

"One curse ended," Demither said

softly, "another begins. Sparr will take me now —"

Ka-foom! The Ninns blasted into the dome once more. Demither's guards rushed to them.

But the Ninns kept coming. Hundreds of them. They charged in, filling the palace.

Keeah turned to the witch. "You said you gave me your powers for a dangerous journey. Tell me now — why did we go to the Upper World?"

The witch's face had changed again. It was now as terrifying as Relna's was beautiful. "You will learn when the time is right, not before!"

Eric looked at Demither's cold expression. He remembered what Om had told him.

Keeah had no memory of it. But together she and Demither had hidden something in the Upper World.

And Om said Eric would find it.

With a final push, hundreds of heavy-footed red warriors blew past Demither's guards and surrounded the witch.

"Sparr wants you now!" the warriors grunted. They quickly threw an iron net over her and pulled her away.

"Beware the sorcerer!" Demither shouted. "He could be anyone! Beware . . . beware!"

Splash!

A dark wave swept into the throne room. On the wave rode the snakey creature with the stubby red snout. It slithered into the throne room, hissing and growling.

"Galen?" said Julie.

"Eerrgh!" the creature growled. Its burning eyes flashed at the children, then it turned and vanished into the dark sea again.

The witch struggled briefly in her net, then was dragged into the darkness by the Ninns.

"I will find you!" Relna called to her sister. "I will never give up hope!"

A moment later, the witch was gone, the Ninns were gone, and the undersea world was quiet, peaceful, and still.

Even Demither's guards had disappeared into the far corners of the green city.

"It is over," said Queen Relna. "We must go."

Linking their hands, Keeah and her mother whispered strange words together. Surrounded by a glistening bubble of air, Queen Relna, Keeah, and the three friends then left the dome and floated away from the witch's realm.

Breaking the surface, they found Friddle's plane — its wings folded up on the sides — rocking gently on the waves.

Darkness was now passing away from the water and the land. The hurricane had vanished.

It seemed like a new day.

"Welcome, Queen Relna, to my humble craft!" the inventor said, helping them aboard, then giving the queen a deep bow. "I was as worried as anything! Besides, the yip-yips were getting quite restless —"

All of a sudden the two blue fur balls jumped out of their cage and — *ploof- ploof!* — instead of yip-yips, two figures appeared before them.

"Galen!" exclaimed Keeah. "And Max!"

"We could not stay away," said the wizard.

"And the only way I could stop him from meddling," chirped Max, "was to go with him!"

"My queen!" said the wizard, bowing his white head. "We are all at your service."

Relna smiled at her old friend. "I see Droon has been in good hands."

"Keeah has indeed done well today," Galen said. "And against such terrible odds!" Then he hugged the princess and her mother tightly.

As he did, Julie stared at him, then at the dark water below, then at Galen again.

"Wait a second . . . if you were up here the whole time, then who was that ugly monster down there —" Julie stopped. She jumped.

"Oh! It was him, wasn't it? It was Sparr! He's even uglier now. And I thought he was you! Oh! I bopped him! I bopped Sparr! With this hand!"

"Julie, don't freak out," said Neal with a grin.

"You'd better wash that hand," said Eric.

Julie plunged it into the water. "Eeew! Yuck!"

Laughing, Keeah turned to her mother. Her smile faded. "Sparr will come back, won't he?"

The queen looked out across the sea. The last of the Ninn ships was disappearing over the horizon. "Yes," she said, "but in what form, we do not know."

"Keeah, you have learned much today," Galen added. "You were tempted by the dark forces but did not bend to them. You have acted far older than your years."

Keeah beamed at first, then frowned. "But does having powers mean I have to grow up? That I can't have fun anymore?"

"Ha!" said the old wizard, smiling under his snow-white beard. "I think you are getting a tiny bit ahead of yourself, Princess. There is still much for you to learn. For instance, Quill wrote something after you left. The legendary Hob has gotten loose again. And we must all go in search of him."

Keeah blinked. "Hob? I never heard of Hob."

Galen grinned. "Of course not — he is one of the best-kept secrets of Droon!"

Neal turned to Eric. "Why do I get the feeling that there are tons of secrets about Droon?"

"And that it will take about a million years to learn them all?" added Julie.

Keeah put her arms around her friends. "I guess this means I'll be seeing you soon."

Eric laughed. "Real soon!"

Max pointed to the nearby coast. The magical staircase was resting on the very top of the cliffs. "Your world calls you back again," he chirped. "At least for a little while."

Friddle giggled. "Which means that I need my yips-yips back! Max? Galen?"

Ploof-ploof! The wizard and his spider troll helper were suddenly blue fur balls again. They hopped into their cage and began to run.

As they did, the plane lifted up over the waves and flew toward the cliffs of Mintar.

The orange sun of afternoon peeked out behind the last few clouds. It shone across the green water and made even Demither's scary realm seem peaceful.

Friddle landed next to the shimmering stairs.

"Farewell, friends of Droon!" said Queen Relna, giving each of the kids a special hug.

"I hope you have sweet dreams," added Keeah. She smiled as they started up the stairs.

Neal ran up the steps first, waving to Keeah and Friddle and Queen Relna.

" 'Bye, yip-yips!" Julie called out.

"Yip! Yip!" said Galen and Max.

"Hey, guys," said Neal, when his friends joined him halfway up the stairs. "How about a nice, normal day of just hanging out? No magic. Just us. What do you say?"

Julie smiled. "A nice, normal day? That sounds soooo good!"

Eric laughed, feeling lighter than air as he chased his friends to the top of the stairs. Then, turning, he raised his hands to wave at Keeah one more time.

That was when he saw the faint blue sparks shooting from the tips of his fingers.

ABOUT THE AUTHOR

Tony Abbott is the author of more than two dozen funny novels for young readers, including the popular *Danger Guys* books and the *Weird Zone* series. Since childhood he has been drawn to stories that challenge the imagination, and, like Eric, Julie, and Neal, he often dreamed of finding doors that open to other worlds. Now that he is older — though not quite as old as Galen Longbeard — he believes he may have found some of those doors. They are called books. Tony Abbott was born in Ohio and now lives with his wife and two daughters in Connecticut.

For more information about Tony Abbott and the continuing saga of Droon, please visit tonyabbottbooks.com.

THE SECRETS OF DROON

By Tony Abbott

Under the stairs, a magical world awaits you!

- ❏ 0-590-10839-5   #1: The Hidden Stairs and the Magic Carpet
- ❏ 0-590-10841-7   #2: Journey to the Volcano Palace
- ❏ 0-590-10840-9   #3: The Mysterious Island
- ❏ 0-590-10842-5   #4: City in the Clouds
- ❏ 0-590-10843-3   #5: The Great Ice Battle
- ❏ 0-590-10844-1   #6: The Sleeping Giant of Goll
- ❏ 0-439-18297-2   #7: Into the Land of the Lost
- ❏ 0-439-18298-0   #8: The Golden Wasp
- ❏ 0-439-20772-X   #9: The Tower of the Elf King
- ❏ 0-439-20784-3   #10: Quest for the Queen
- ❏ 0-439-20785-1   #11: The Hawk Bandits of Tarkoom
- ❏ 0-439-20786-X   #12: Under the Serpent Sea
- ❏ 0-439-30606-X   #13: The Mask of Maliban
- ❏ 0-439-30607-8   #14: Voyage of the *Jaffa Wind*
- ❏ 0-439-30608-6   #15: The Moon Scroll
- ❏ 0-439-30609-4   #16: The Knights of Silversnow
- ❏ 0-439-42078-4   #17: Dream Thief
- ❏ 0-439-42079-2   #18: Search for the Dragon Ship
- ❏ 0-439-42080-6   #19: The Coiled Viper
- ❏ 0-439-56040-3   #20: In the Ice Caves of Krog
- ❏ 0-439-56043-8   #21: Flight of the Genie
- ❏ 0-439-56048-9   #22: The Isle of Mists
- ❏ 0-439-66157-9   #23: The Fortress of the Treasure Queen
- ❏ 0-439-66158-7   #24: The Race to Doobesh
- ❏ 0-439-67173-6   #25: The Riddle of Zorfendorf Castle
- ❏ 0-439-42077-6   Special Edition #1: The Magic Escapes $5.99
- ❏ 0-439-56049-7   Special Edition #2: Wizard or Witch? $5.99

$3.99 each!

Available Wherever You Buy Books or Use This Order Form

Scholastic Inc., P.O. Box 7502, Jefferson City, MO 65102

Please send me the books I have checked above. I am enclosing $_____ (please add $2.00 to cover shipping and handling). Send check or money order—no cash or C.O.D.s please.

Name_____Birth date_____

Address_____

City_____State/Zip_____

Please allow four to six weeks for delivery. Offer good in U.S.A. only. Sorry, mail orders are not available to residents of Canada. Prices subject to change.

scholastic.com/droon   ■ **SCHOLASTIC**

SCHOLASTIC and associated logos are trademarks and/or registered trademarks of Scholastic Inc.

SODBL0505